ALYSSA DELLE PALME

Evernight Teen ®

www.evernightteen.com

Copyright© 2023

Alyssa Delle Palme

ISBN: 978-0-3695-0904-8

Cover Artist: Jay Aheer

Editor: CA Clauson

ALYSSA DELLE PALME

DEDICATION

For my mother, Meg, for instilling a deep appreciation for nature and love of reading.

ALYSSA DELLE PALME

.

Alyssa Delle Palme

Copyright © 2023

❮❮·•◆•·❯❯

Chapter One

Summer 1999

"Don't puke in the car."

Sarah's mom, Alice, kept one hand on the steering wheel while the other searched for something in the glove box.

"Mom! You're swerving!" said Sarah's older sister, Mabel.

"Sorry, I was looking for a paper bag." Mom placed her hands back on the steering wheel at ten and two and glanced at Sarah in the rearview mirror. "Your face is pale. If you're going to be sick, I can pull over."

In the back of their silver Ford Taurus, Sarah was sandwiched between Mabel and a leaning tower of sleeping bags and pillows. Their West Highland Terrier, Pete, panted in the front passenger seat, and his hot salmon breath drifted into Sarah's perspiring face. The dog rode shotgun because if he sat anywhere else in the car, he'd lose his lunch. Motion sickness ran in the family.

"Honey, maybe your stomach is unsettled because you're upset that Grandma isn't going to be at the cottage this summer," Mom said.

Sarah missed her grandmother terribly, they all did, but she was fairly certain it was her mother's lead foot that had brought on this queasiness. That or all the bends and curves in the dirt road that were guiding them to Pine Lake. Sarah stared out the window at the passing corn fields. Her grandma used to join them for the drive up to the cottage. She was a tall woman with a smart white bob haircut, and striking blue eyes. She was always impeccably dressed. In the summer, she donned linen pants, striped button-down shirts, and a straw bucket hat. Grandma had always made Mom stop at the halfway point, which was *The Doughnut Hole Bakery*, because she needed to use the washroom. Grandma always returned to the car with a box of freshly baked sugar doughnuts and a couple of small cartons of chocolate milk for her and Mabel.

"Grandma wouldn't want you to be upset," said Mom as she drove straight past the bakery. "She would want you to enjoy your summer at the lake."

Sarah nodded. She knew Mom just wanted to help, but Sarah hoped her mother would take her own advice to heart. Her mom hadn't been the same since her grandma died. Once a health nut who walked five kilometers every morning and drank green juice for breakfast, Mom could now be found on the couch every afternoon with Pete curled up in her lap, a bowl of plain potato chips in hand and *Dr. Phil* on the TV. Sarah tried to tell her dad her concerns over the phone, but he had shrugged her off.

"Your mother is grieving," said her dad. "It's all part of the process."

"I've never seen her like this," whispered Sarah. "Maybe you should come home."

"I'm in the middle of an important work project. I can't leave. Who do you think is going to pay for your tuition in the fall?"

"I know. I'm just worried about her."

"Sarah, I have a two-week vacation booked for the beginning of July. I fly out of Vancouver in a few weeks, and the plan is to meet you all at the cottage."

"She misses you, you know. She—"

"Sarah, hun, I have to run. My boss is calling me on the other line. Everything is going to be okay. We'll talk soon." Click.

Sarah's dad was born and raised in a small town in British Columbia along the Sunshine Coast. When the Canadian government offered him a contract position in his home province, he jumped at the opportunity and accepted the job before talking it through with Sarah's mom.

"You're leaving?" Her mom was furious with him when he told her.

"It's only for six months."

He'd begged Mom to join him, enticing her with ideas of romantic walks on the beach and fresh seafood for dinner every night of the week, but her mom wouldn't do that to Sarah. She refused to uproot their youngest daughter in her last year of high school. So, Alice and Sarah had stayed behind, and Mabel had gone off to university.

At the memory of her dad leaving, Sarah felt an

acidic burn rise in her chest. "Mom, can you roll down the windows?" she asked. Her mom kept her foot on the gas and her eyes on the winding road as she pressed all four black power window switches.

"Stop being so dramatic," said Mabel as gusts of fresh country air blew through the open windows, tossing her long, wavy blonde hair in all directions. Sarah took a deep breath in through her nose and zipped her lips shut. She wasn't feeling up to a confrontation with Mabel. Besides, she knew her sister's snotty attitude had nothing to do with her.

****

A few weeks ago, when Mabel returned home from her second year away at university, she went straight to her room and slammed the door. Mom had spent the entire day preparing a roast beef dinner in anticipation of Mabel's arrival.

"I can't wait to have both my girls under the same roof again," she had said.

Her mom had even stopped by the farmer's market to pick up fresh local asparagus for the occasion. The green, butter-braised spears became soggy in their sauce as Sarah and her mom waited for their guest of honor to join their "welcome home" celebration.

"Mabel?" Sarah said. She gently knocked on her sister's bedroom door. "Dinner is ready."

"I'm not hungry."

"Mom made your favorite. She went to a lot of work to—"

"I said I'm not hungry!"

"Brat," muttered Sarah as she stomped back down the stairs. "Mabel isn't hungry," Sarah told her mom.

"Oh, dear." Mom took off her stained, floral apron and hung it up in the tiny kitchen pantry. "I'll go talk to her."

Sarah sat down at the dining room table. After a while, she served herself a heaping mound of mashed potatoes and sprinkled them with pepper. She couldn't believe Mabel's immature behavior. She was twenty years old, for Pete's sake! Their mother had gone to a lot of work to prepare a nice supper for Mabel, which wasn't easy for her. Some days, Mom wouldn't leave the house because she was too overwhelmed with grief. Sarah shoveled a fork full of cold mashed potato into her mouth, but it slid down her throat like glue. She brought her plate to the kitchen and dumped her leftovers into the compost bin. Sarah opened the fridge and saw the homemade chocolate cake Mom had baked for dessert. She grabbed the cake and a sharp knife and cut straight through her mom's perfectly written *Welcome Home Mabel* message in white vanilla icing. Sarah took her dessert into the family room, slapped her bare feet on top of the wooden coffee table, and flipped on the TV. A rerun of *Clueless* was playing. When Mom finally made her way back downstairs, she cut herself a piece of chocolate cake, poured a glass of red wine, and joined Sarah on the couch.

"Benny broke up with Mabel," whispered Mom.

Sarah stopped lifting her fork halfway to her mouth. "What? Why?"

"He said he didn't want to do the long distance anymore."

"But they've been together for years! Do you think he met someone else?"

Mom shrugged.

Sarah stared at the TV. "I'm shocked!" Mabel and Benny were high school sweethearts and had been together since they were fifteen. He was at their house so often, he was like an annoying older brother to Sarah. "What an asshole."

Mom took a sip of wine. "Your sister is devastated. She's still grieving the loss of Grandma, too."

"I can't believe it. What surprises me the most is that it was Benny who broke up with Mabel."

Mabel and Benny were one of those couples where one partner is significantly more attractive than the other. Not only was Mabel gorgeous, but she was smart, too. Top of her class at the University of Toronto and well on her way to becoming a biologist. Benny, on the other hand, had been rejected from the Police Foundations program at the community college. He'd settled for a part-time bartender gig in downtown Ottawa. It wasn't just his resumé that was unattractive. Whenever he laughed, it reminded Sarah of an excited stallion.

After the breakup, Mabel barely left her room, which unsettled their mom. She fussed around the house, not only preparing and packing for their trip to the cottage for the summer, but she acted as Mabel's nursemaid. She made her homemade soups and smoothies and left them outside her bedroom door on a breakfast tray. She even flipped through several self-help books and folded down the corners of pages she thought Mabel would find helpful.

"I'm worried Mabel won't come to the cottage," Mom said, dropping an overripe banana into the blender.

Sarah hated seeing her mother riddled with anxiety. "Mabel's just being dramatic."

Mom added a splash of orange juice into the blender. "All she needs to get over the breakup is to spend the summer at the lake. Grandma always said it was a healing place."

When it was time to leave, Sarah breathed a sigh of relief when Mabel emerged from her room. She had never understood what Mabel saw in Benny anyway.

"You're better off without him," Sarah said in an

attempt to console Mabel. "You deserve better."

Mabel instantly shut her down. "What would you know about it?" she seethed. "You've never been in a serious relationship."

At eighteen years old, Sarah had never had a boyfriend. She'd dated a few guys from high school, but none of them gave her that uncontrollable desire to be around them.

"Are you a lesbian?" her best friend, Julie, asked one Sunday afternoon as the girls flipped through *Seventeen* magazines on top of Sarah's queen-size bed.

"No," said Sarah. She skimmed an article about cellulite remedies. "Why?"

"Because Derrick is the hottest guy in school, and you turned him down."

"Derrick may be good-looking, but he's incredibly dull."

"Aw, but the way he followed you around at the grad party, I felt sorry for him."

Sarah had tried her best to avoid Derrick, but like the stink of a skunk, she couldn't get rid of him. At their prom after-party, Sarah and Julie were standing at an island in the host's kitchen when Derrick had come up behind them and dropped his athletic arms around both their shoulders.

"Hey, ladies," he said, looking left to right, "are we having a good time?" The three of them watched in awe as their classmate, Greg, chugged a beer with a funnel. When Greg was finished, he wiped the white foam from his lips with the back of his hand and everyone in the kitchen cheered.

"I can't believe Patrick Lee's parents invited the entire senior class to their house for an after-party," said Julie, peering closely at Derrick's perfect jawline.

"I know, it's wild," he said. Derrick took his arm

off Julie's shoulder and grabbed a handful of Bits & Bites from a bowl on the counter and tossed them into his mouth. Sarah shook her head. She didn't understand what Julie saw in him.

"I've been looking for you all night," he said as he turned his attention to Sarah. His teeth were stained orange from the party snacks. "Can I get you a beer?"

"No thanks, I'm good with water," she said. Sarah tried to reach for her Aquafina bottle on top of the island, but it was impossible to move with his vice grip on her shoulders.

"Let me take you out," he said.

"I can't, Derrick. I already told you I'm going to my grandmother's cottage for the summer."

"There's still tonight," he whispered in her ear. "I'm so hot for you, baby."

"Derrick, stop." She tried to push him away to no avail.

"Sorry to interrupt," said Julie as she poked her face between Derrick and Sarah, "but our ride is here. Time to go." Sarah gave Julie an appreciative look and ducked out from under Derrick's stranglehold.

The girls walked arm in arm towards the front door. "Thank you," said Sarah.

"I had to do something. You looked like a startled baby bunny. You do realize that every girl at that party would kill to be in your position, right?"

"They can have him," Sarah said. "His breath smelled like old cheddar."

Sarah wasn't interested in Derrick, or anyone else from their high school for that matter. Only one guy had ever sparked a happy tickle inside her chest that intensified every time she saw him. No guy could hold a candle to her crush, Scott Roberts.

****

Sarah groaned as her mother hit yet another bump in the road, as if she were playing whack-a-mole with all the potholes. When they passed by a century-old stone church and cemetery, Sarah held her breath. Her grandma once told her that if she didn't hold her breath as they passed by a graveyard, spirits would fly up her nose. Sarah knew her grandma was probably just teasing her, but even at eighteen, she wasn't taking any chances. Afterall, Grandma had been a devout Catholic. Sarah grew lightheaded and shut her eyes tight to stop the spins.

"Look, we're almost there," said Mabel.

Sarah opened her eyes just as Mom drove up the last hill that would bring them to their cozy retreat for the summer. The familiar scent of the pine trees helped to settle Sarah's stomach. Once they reached the top of the hill, her mom slowed down and gently rolled past a rusty orange cottage that belonged to the Roberts family. Sarah perked up when she saw her lifelong friend, Jeff Roberts, sitting on the steps of the front porch. He smiled his goofy grin and waved when he saw their Ford Taurus roll up.

"Hey, loser!" Sarah yelled through the window, "did you miss me?"

"Did I ever," said Jeff as he jogged toward their car. "Welcome back, ladies. You're looking well, Mrs. Williams. I was so sorry to hear about your mother's passing."

"Thank you, Jeffrey," said Mom. She tucked a delicate lock of blonde hair behind her ear. "I received the beautiful flower arrangement your family sent."

"It's going to be such a different summer without her here," he said. "Who is going to yell at us when we build our bonfires too big?"

Mom laughed out loud for the first time in months, and Sarah suddenly realized her mother had barely cracked a smile since Grandma died. It warmed her heart to hear her mom's belly laugh again. Leave it to Jeff to have everyone in stitches.

"Even at ninety years old, she was a spitfire," said Mom. She wiped away a happy tear from her soft cheek. "Where is your brother?"

"Scott's lifeguarding at the public beach again this summer. He'll be back later tonight."

Just hearing Scott's name sparked that happy tickle inside Sarah's chest. She'd never told anyone about her feelings for Scott, not even Julie, and she never would. Sarah had spent every summer with the Roberts brothers since they were all in diapers. She had always been just "one of the guys," a low maintenance girl who they could joke around with. She was also privy to their dating histories, and Scott had a long list of conquests. Women couldn't resist his curly dark hair and charming smile.

"Tell Scott 'hey' for us," piped up Mabel. Sarah looked over at her sister in surprise. Mabel had barely muttered three words to anyone since her breakup with Benny.

"For sure," said Jeff. "You guys should come by once you've settled in. I want to introduce you to my friend from school. He's staying with us for the summer."

"Oh, how nice," said Mom. "How was your first year at St. Francis Xavier?"

"It was unreal. Nova Scotians sure know how to party. My mom is just relieved I passed all my classes." Jeff was like the Prince Harry of his family, the wild and fun younger brother.

"Tell your parents I say 'hello.' Jack is on a six-month contract in British Columbia, but he's flying here in a couple of weeks for vacation. When he's back, we'll have to have them over for cocktails on the deck."

"I'll tell them, Mrs. Williams."

"See you around," said Sarah. Her mother took her foot off the brake and continued down the dirt road to their neighboring cottage. Mom maneuvered the Taurus to the right side of the road when a young man, who looked like he had stepped off the pages of an Abercrombie ad, jogged passed them toward the Roberts' cottage.

"Who is that?" said Mabel. All three women turned and stared at the ridiculously handsome jogger.

"Do you think he's Jeff's friend from school?" said Sarah. She was intrigued. The mystery man didn't spark that happy tickle inside her chest, but he certainly made her stomach flip. They watched as he turned into the Roberts' driveway.

"That's a lot of beefcake," said Mom as she drove into the driveway of their cottage. Sarah looked at Mabel, and they burst into a fit of giggles.

"Summer just got a whole lot hotter," agreed Mabel.

ALYSSA DELLE PALME

Chapter Two

Sarah's heart sank when she walked through the front door of the cottage. Straight ahead in the master bedroom, Grandma's slippers were placed neatly beside the foot of her bed. Grandma's old green cottage sweatshirt, a souvenir from a trip to Prince Edward Island to see *Anne of Green Gables: The Musical*, hung all alone on a hook on her bedroom wall. Sarah swallowed the lump in her throat and adjusted the heavy duffle bag on her shoulder. She made her way to the kitchen. The cottage was small and minimalist by design but felt spacious inside because the large windows gave it an open, airy feel.

"When your grandfather built this cottage, he wanted to make it feel like you were one with nature," her grandma had told her one summer afternoon over a game of Scrabble. Sarah's grandfather died before she was born, and she loved to listen to her grandma tell stories about him.

"Your grandfather was ten years old when his father sent him out onto the land with his dog and a shotgun," she said. Her arthritic hands shook as she placed the word "squirrel" across the Scrabble board. 87 points.

"How long did he have to stay out there for?" Sarah asked.

"A couple of days."

Sarah couldn't imagine sleeping in the forest all by herself. "Was he scared?"

Grandma reached into the velvet Scrabble bag, collected new letters, and added them to the wooden rack. "I would imagine so."

"Why would his father make him do something

like that?"

"He wanted him to be self-sufficient. When your grandfather was a boy, his family would leave their home every summer to live in a cabin that had no running water, no electricity, and no indoor bathroom."

"That sounds awful."

"Well, it was important to your great-grandfather that his children learn to appreciate the comforts of their home."

"Is that why Grandpa created a set of rules for our cottage?" Sarah asked.

Her grandmother nodded. When Sarah's grandfather had built their cottage in the 1960s, he had created a list of rules for his family to follow: no motorboats, no television, and no telephone.

"Grandpa believed if you took the time to teach children to appreciate nature, you would be giving them a gift they would have forever," said Grandma.

Decades later, the Williams family still abided by most of his rules. Grandma broke the "no telephone" rule the summer Mabel had her accident. It happened when Sarah was eight and Mabel was ten. Their cottage was like a treehouse that sat high in the forest at the edge of a cliff. To get down to the lake, you had to descend forty stairs. It always took some time for them to build their stamina as they went up and down the stairs multiple times a day. Sarah and Mabel liked to climb the old pine tree that grew out of the mossy rock face beside the deck. From there, they could see the Roberts' cottage. A small pine grove divided their cottages and provided some privacy, but high up in the tree, they could spy on Jeff and Scott.

The summer that Mabel was hurt, they had invented a game called "elevator," where they would grab onto the highest branch they could reach with their hands and bounce on a lower branch with their feet. One day, Mabel bounced on a branch that was too weak, and it snapped. She fell straight down, past the deck, and landed on a rough rug of pine needles below.

"Mom!" Sarah screamed. She scrambled out of the tree to get help. Her dad was still in the city for work and her grandma was going to ride up with him to the cottage on the weekend. Sarah found her mother on the dock by the lake. She was working on her summer tan. "Mabel fell out of the elevator tree, and I heard her leg crack," she cried.

"Go get Mr. Draper!" Her mother quickly climbed up the stairs to Mabel. "He'll know what to do."

Mr. Draper, a retired army medic, and his wife owned a cottage across the bay of the lake. Sarah sprinted down the dirt road like Olympian Donovan Bailey. Even when she got a side stitch, she didn't stop running. Sarah worried he wouldn't be home and she wouldn't know what to do next. When she arrived ten minutes later, she found Mr. Draper outside chopping wood. He yelled at his wife to grab the first aid kit and the three of them jumped into his station wagon.

Mabel wailed like a wounded animal when he placed her bruised leg into a splint. Mr. Draper had built the brace himself with two straight tree branches and yellow rope. But then Mabel became eerily quiet and barely whimpered when Mr. Draper picked her up and gently placed her in the back of his station wagon to take her to the hospital.

"Sarah, stay with Mrs. Draper and be good," said her mother. She kissed Sarah on the forehead and climbed into the back of the station wagon with Mabel.

Mrs. Draper made Sarah a can of Campbell's tomato soup and a grilled cheese sandwich for supper. Her mother and Mr. Draper didn't return until the next morning.

"She broke her femur," said Mom, sobbing. "They put her in a full body cast from her chest down. She's going to be in the hospital for a couple of weeks."

A phone was installed in their cottage a few days later.

Sarah longed to call Julie, but the phone was only supposed to be used for emergencies. All cellphones were kept in a wicker basket on top of the fridge. There was no cell reception on the lake anyway. The light-colored pine floors creaked as Sarah walked through the open living area toward the two back bedrooms. The simple Scandinavian décor inside was calming and comforting. The black stand-alone woodstove was a nice contrast to the white shipboard paneled walls. Sarah dropped her duffle bag onto the gray couch next to the marigold throw pillows.

"I've decided to stay in Grandma's room this summer," her mom announced.

"I call our bedroom," said Mabel. She rolled her suitcase into the middle bedroom and shut the door. Sarah's shoulders slumped forward.

"Don't take it personally," said Mom. She put her arm around Sarah and gave her shoulder a squeeze. "She just needs some space. Why don't you take my old room? The queen-size bed will be much more comfortable than the bunk beds."

Sarah gave her mother a half-smile. She picked up her duffle bag and walked into the back bedroom, her refuge for the summer. Pete followed her in and sniffed around the room. He lifted his white furry leg and marked his territory in the middle of the floor.

"Mom! Pete just peed in my room!"

A minute later, Mom walked into Sarah's room armed with Windex and a roll of paper towel. Sarah sat at the edge of the bed and watched as her mother cleaned up the yellow puddle. "Do you think Julie could come up to the cottage for a visit?"

"Oh, I don't know. I thought it would be nice to spend the summer together, just us."

"Dad isn't here, Mabel mopes around and barely speaks to me, and you're in bed by 8:30 every night."

"You want Julie to come here?" said Mabel. She leaned against the doorframe to Sarah's new room and peered inside.

"Yes, I'd like to spend more time with her before we both go away to school in the fall."

"No way," said Mabel. She crossed her arms across her chest. "It's supposed to be just family this summer."

"This is none of your business," said Sarah.

"Now girls—"

"It is my business," said Mabel.

"Just forget I asked," Sarah muttered.

She stood up from the bed and stormed past her mother and Mabel. She marched to the back of the cottage, opened the sliding glass door, and stepped onto the deck that overlooked the lake. The sunshine splashed across the water and made it sparkle like Canada Dry ginger ale. A cool breeze soothed Sarah's burning cheeks. She took a thin black elastic from around her wrist and tied her long brown hair into a ponytail. Not ready to face Mabel or her mother, Sarah snuck around the side of the cottage and walked down the driveway toward the dirt road.

Sarah's legs were restless from the long car ride, and they begged to burn off some pent-up energy. A walk would do her good. When Sarah reached the Roberts' cottage, Scott's black truck with a Queens University bumper sticker was parked in the driveway. She picked up her pace and stared straight ahead. She wasn't prepared to run into Scott. She was wearing old denim cut-offs and a baggy white T-shirt that did nothing for her figure. Sarah moved swiftly down the big hill. When she reached the bottom, she noticed crumbs of mica scattered all over the road.

"Mica is a mineral that was used in the old days to insulate the windows in stove heaters," her grandma told her one summer on an early morning walk.

Sarah liked how mica sparkled in the sun like glitter. Sarah and her grandma were the early birds of the family and would often wake up at the crack of dawn. While the rest of their family slept in, Sarah and her grandma would tiptoe out of the cottage and take off on an adventure together. Sarah liked to pick wildflowers on their hikes, and when they returned to the cottage for breakfast, her grandma would place her bouquet in a mason jar of water and proudly display them on the picnic table.

Sarah stopped walking when she reached the abandoned mica mine, which was hidden among the trees near the road. Through the dense brush, she could see the outline of the deep quarry. Down at her feet were some daisies, her grandma's favorite flower. She smiled and was bending down to pick some when Jeff and his friend jogged around a bend in the road. Sarah stood up straight and waved to her friend as the young men slowed their strides and approached her.

"Hey!" said Jeff, out of breath. "Where are you off to?"

"Nowhere special. Just out for a walk. Is this your second run of the day?" she asked Jeff's friend directly.

"I'm sorry," panted Jeff. "Sarah, this is my friend, Hugo."

Hugo flashed Sarah a gorgeous, crooked smile.

"Hey. It's very nice to meet you," he said.

"Nice to meet you, too." She smiled. "Where are you from? I can't place your accent."

"Switzerland. I wish someone had told me how hard it was to get a Canadian accent when I started learning English."

Sarah giggled. She liked his sense of humor.

"Yeah, right. All the ladies find his accent irresistible, and this guy loves the attention," Jeff told Sarah.

"You speak English very well," she said.

Hugo's accent was faint. Sarah thought it was endearing the way he pronounced his "ws" like "vs," like when he said he was from "Svitzerland." Hugo took off his Nike baseball cap and ran a large hand through his shaggy, dirty-blond hair. Sweat ran down his chest and between his abs. It wasn't just his accent that Sarah found inherently sexy.

"So, you two are friends from school?" she asked.

"Yeah. Hugo is my teammate. We played for the St. Francis X-Men, and we have to keep in shape for hockey tryouts in the fall."

"Welcome to Pine Lake, Hugo. Are you here for the entire summer?"

"Yes. It was too expensive to fly back home for the break."

"He's staying with us for the summer," said Jeff. "So, listen, my parents have to drive back to the city for a couple of days." He grinned mischievously. "We've invited a few people over for a bonfire tonight. An official kickoff to summer. You have to come."

"For sure," said Sarah. "I'll swing by when I see the campfire going."

"Great!" he said. He leaned over and gave Sarah a swift peck on the cheek before he and Hugo took off in a full sprint toward the big hill.

Show-offs, Sarah thought. She added Lily of the Valley to her bouquet, making sure to leave enough wildflowers behind for the bees. As Sarah hiked back to the cottage with flowers in hand, she had an extra pep in her step.

Sarah walked through the front door of the cottage and found her mother fast asleep on her grandma's bed in the master bedroom. Pete was curled up on the pillow beside her, happy to partake in a late afternoon nap. Sarah reached for the chunky beige knit blanket at the foot of the bed, and when she gently laid it out on top of her mother, her mom opened her sleepy eyes.

"I was just resting my eyes," Mom whispered. "What time is it?"

"5:00," Sarah said softly. She sat down beside her mother on the edge of the bed.

"Listen honey, I've thought about it, and you can invite Julie up to the cottage for a visit."

"Really?"

"Yes, you've had a difficult year with grandma's passing and your dad not being around. You need your best friend."

Sarah looked at her mother. The deepening creases around her tired blue eyes reminded Sarah of her mother's fragility.

"But, what about Mabel?"

"Don't worry. I've already talked to Mabel. Julie is around so much, she is practically part of this family," she said. She offered Sarah a weak smile and gently patted her bare knee. "Now, I better get up and finish getting supper ready."

"Anything I can do to help?"

"You could set the table."

Sarah walked into the kitchen and placed her

wildflowers into a mason jar of cold water. She looked out the sliding glass door to see Mabel peeling corn on the deck. As their mom set to work on wrapping the baked potatoes in aluminum foil, Sarah grabbed the utensils and three plates and went outside to set the picnic table.

"I ran into Jeff and his hot friend," Sarah told Mabel to break the ice. Her sister sat up straighter.

"What was he like?"

"He was nice. His name is Hugo, and he's from Switzerland. He has the most adorable accent."

"No way! Just when you think he couldn't get any hotter…"

"Mr. and Mrs. Roberts have to go into the city for a few days, so the guys are throwing a bonfire tonight. Do you want to go with me?"

"Yes," Mabel said, accepting the olive branch. "I could use a night out."

At dinner, Sarah shoveled forkfuls of buttery potato into her mouth and washed it down with an ice-cold glass of lemonade before she excused herself. She was eager to get ready for the bonfire. She laid two potential outfits out on her white duvet, a pale pink cotton summer dress or her favorite pair of Levis paired with a button-up plaid shirt. She chose the dress and styled it with an oversize white cardigan and her brown Birkenstocks. She didn't want Scott to think she was too eager. She took her long brown hair out of its ponytail and let it fall loosely over her shoulders. She searched her makeup bag for the coffee-colored Covergirl eyeshadow palette and applied a neutral satin base to her eyelids with a gold shimmer finish to highlight her big brown eyes. She coated her lashes with a light layer of mascara and dabbed some clear gloss on her lips. When she was ready, she walked across the hall and knocked on her old bedroom door. "Mabel?"

"Be out in a minute!"

Sarah waited in the open living area. Her mother was curled up on the gray couch with an Oprah's Book Club book in hand. Pete rested at her feet. A pang of guilt hit Sarah in her lower stomach. "Are you going to be okay here all alone, Mom?"

"I'm not alone. I have Pete. Go and have fun with your sister. I'm going to turn in soon anyway."

Sarah kissed her mom on the cheek and stepped out the sliding glass door onto the deck. She looked out at the lake and took a deep breath. Rich scents of smoke and burning birch wood wafted over from the campfire at the Roberts' cottage. The lake shimmered under the setting sun, and a gentle breeze drifted through the trees. Sarah shivered, not because she was cold, but because she was both nervous and excited to see Scott.

Chapter Three

The campfire burned brightly as Sarah and Mabel arrived at the Roberts' cottage. Sarah was surprised to see how many people the guys had invited over and only recognized a few summer kids from the cottages around the lake.

The others must be townies.

Big red Adirondack chairs sat empty around the campfire. Most of the guests were gathered around the keg and the makeshift food table that the guys had set up. Sarah was impressed with their spread—veggie trays with spicy hummus, charcuterie boards decorated with cheese, meat, crackers, olives, fancy mustard, and pickled carrots. Overhead, pretty strings of twinkle lights hung across the trees and illuminated the outdoor space. Fireflies flashed in the forest, like tiny magicians that appeared and disappeared in the blink of an eye.

"You made it!" Jeff called out to them. He left the group that was gathered around the keg and welcomed Sarah and Mabel with a warm kiss on the cheek. "Let me get you a drink."

"I can get one myself, thanks," said Mabel. She smiled at Jeff and squeezed Sarah's hand before she walked toward the group of people gathered at the keg.

"Coke for me, please," said Sarah.

Jeff sat down in one of the big Adirondack chairs and reached into a cooler beside him. Sarah sat down across from him and graciously accepted a dripping ice-cold can of Coca-Cola. She took a small sip of the sweet bubbly drink.

"I've missed you," she said. "Tell me everything. Did you meet anyone special at school this year?"

"Between my courses and hockey, I didn't really have time for a girlfriend. I mean, I did have some fun." He winked.

"Of course, you did," she laughed.

"You're going to love going away to school. I heard Concordia's writing program is one of the best in the country. Congratulations."

"To be honest, I'm a little nervous."

Jeff reached into the cooler and grabbed a brown bottle of Labatt Blue. "I get it. When my parents dropped me off at university last fall, it felt like they had thrown me into the deep end of a pool and told me to learn how to swim. It's the unknown that gets you. Trust me, Sarah, university is a pretty great place."

Sarah looked into Jeff's friendly blue eyes and smiled. He always knew the right thing to say. They spent the next hour catching up and feeding the fire. The dry logs crackled and hissed, releasing their intoxicating sweet aroma in the smoke. A couple of new guests arrived at the bonfire, and Jeff got up to greet them. Sarah kept watch over the fire and scanned the party, looking for Scott. Mabel was still at the keg with two red cups in hand, but Scott was nowhere to be seen. She took another sip of Coke and looked into the pine grove that separated their cottages. She could make out the remnants of the fort they had built when they were kids.

"Help me with this dead branch," Jeff had said to Sarah one summer afternoon when she was ten.

"What are we going to do with it?"

"We're going to build a lean-to shelter."

Jeff always had the best ideas. They had worked together all summer on their top-secret fort. They gathered fallen branches from the forest and cleared the debris at the base of an old pine tree. Jeff and Sarah leaned the large sticks all around the tree at a 45-degree angle until they had built a robust circular wall with an opening for a door. Next, they gathered small twigs, fallen leaves, and moss to pack into the cracks. Mabel and Scott would help them from time to time, but Sarah and Jeff built most of the fort on their own. It became their sacred place.

After showing his new guests how to pour the perfect cup of beer from the keg, Jeff returned to the campfire.

"Do you remember the treasure maps we used to draw in our fort?" Sarah asked.

Jeff looked into the forest and smiled. "Hell, yeah, I do. We hid Happy Meal toys all over this place."

They looked at each other and burst into laughter. They laughed so hard tears streamed down their cheeks.

"Do you remember how we used to set up booby traps?" she said.

Sarah and Jeff would dig shallow holes near the entrance of their fort and cover them with sticks and leaves. If someone stepped in one, it alerted them that an uninvited guest had been in their fort.

Scott stepped into the firelight, beer in hand. "I almost sprained my ankle in one of your death traps."

Sarah wiped away her tears with the back of her hand, careful not to smudge her mascara. "Hi, Scott." She smiled as she stood up to greet him. He enveloped her in a big bear hug. She nestled her face into his neck and breathed in his scent. He smelled clean, like crisp, fresh sheets.

"Look at you," he said as he placed his hands on her shoulders. "You're all grown up."

Sarah blushed and looked down at her feet.

"Don't embarrass our poor girl," said Jeff. He rose out of his chair and stood beside Scott. Next to his brother, Jeff looked boyish. Scott was taller, more rugged.

"I'm going to go get another drink. Can I get you anything?" said Jeff.

Sarah shook her head no. Jeff walked toward Mabel and the others gathered around the keg.

"I heard you're headed to Montreal in the fall," said Scott. "Congratulations! Your first step to becoming the next Judy Blume."

"I can't believe you remember who my favorite author is." She felt her heart flutter in her chest.

"Of course, I do. You had your nose stuck in one of her books every summer for as long as I can remember."

Sarah felt a shudder of humiliation and quickly changed the subject. "How's Queens? It must feel good to be halfway through your prestigious Education degree."

"Well, the workload is tough. And my 'prestigious' degree will be irrelevant if I'm not a good teacher."

"You will be," Sarah said matter of fact.

She already knew Scott was an excellent teacher. The summer Sarah turned thirteen, her grandma had registered her for the Bronze Medallion Lifesaving course at the public beach. On the first day of the program, Sarah was happily surprised to see Scott in her class. They partnered up for all the rescue drills, and Scott would help her practice different tows and carries off the Roberts' dock. Sarah struggled with the brick test, which was a 15-meter swim out into the lake and a ten-foot dive to the bottom to retrieve a heavy yellow brick. The pressure underwater made it feel like her ears were going to explode.

"Dive down headfirst, Sarah. It will get you there faster," Scott instructed. He worked with her until she was comfortable with the drill. She passed the test with flying colors.

Every summer, Sarah and Scott would register for another level of certification until they earned their National Lifeguard badges. During the school year, Sarah had worked at her community pool.

"Jeff said you're lifeguarding at the public beach again this summer."

"Yeah. It's good money."

"Oh, come on. We both know you only take the job because it's an easy way to pick up women." Sarah nudged him playfully with her elbow.

Scott chuckled. Sarah couldn't help but stare at the dimple in his chin. He wore his cleft chin well.

"Well, my boss, Kurt, can be a dick, but everyone else is cool. Do you need a summer job? I could put in a good word for you."

"You would do that for me?"

"Of course." Scott smiled. His eyes scanned her face, as though he were trying to read her. Scott cleared his throat. "I mean, I'm happy to help out my kid brother's best friend. Just say the word and I'll—"

"Scotty!" Mabel interrupted. She stumbled over to the campfire and threw her arm around his neck.

"Mabel, hi," he said. He leaned in to give her a friendly side hug and was caught off guard when she wrapped both arms around his neck and nuzzled her face into his chest.

"Mmm, you smell good, Scotty."

"Uh, thanks," he said as he gently unwrapped himself from her boa-constrictor grip. "Looks like you found the keg all right."

"And the Fireball shots!" Mabel tried to take another sip of beer from her red plastic cup, but the foam dribbled down the sides of her mouth and onto her t-shirt.

"You want to get out of here?" she slurred. Mabel smiled at Scott with half-opened eyes.

Scott slowly stepped aside and grabbed another log from a nearby wood pile. "Sorry, I have to man the fire tonight." Scott added another log to the pile of red-hot coals.

Sarah stared at her sister in disbelief. This sloppy behavior was so unlike her. Mabel's blonde hair was matted against her forehead, and the front of her t-shirt was all wet.

"Mabel, do you want to go to the food table and grab something to eat?" Sarah suggested. She held on to Mabel's elbow to help steady her.

"I'm not hungry."

"Well, maybe we should go home," Sarah said through gritted teeth. "I think you've had enough."

"Oh, screw off! Get your hands off me." Mabel jerked her arm free.

Sarah watched with wide eyes as her sister wobbled away toward the keg.

"What was that about?" said Scott.

Sarah avoided eye contact and twirled her long hair around her right index finger. Her eyes were brimming with tears. "It was nice talking to you, Scott. I'll see you around."

"Sarah, wait—"

But she didn't. Everyone at the party had heard Mabel yell at her. Sarah's face was burning as everyone stared. She flashed the group a false smile as she quickly passed by the food table and hurried down the steep wooden steps to the Roberts' dock. When she reached the bottom, she took a deep breath. She soaked in the quiet for a moment before the eerie, beautiful call of a loon reminded her that she wasn't alone. She kicked off her Birkenstocks, sat at the edge of the dock, and dipped her pedicured blue cotton-candy toes into the lake. A shooting star flew across the night sky, like a sparkler that had ignited and burst into life.

"The meteor shower is supposed to peak tonight," her grandma had read from the newspaper one summer morning. "You could see over fifty shooting stars tonight."

"That's a lot of wishes," said Sarah, who was eleven years old at the time.

Later that night, Sarah, Mabel, Scott, and Jeff put on their bathing suits and headlamps and ran down to the Roberts' dock.

"Last one in is a rotten egg," yelled Jeff. He jumped in first and swam for the raft that was anchored in the middle of the bay. Mabel followed suit. Scott was about to jump in next when he turned and waited for Sarah.

"Scott, I'm scared," she whispered.

"Don't worry. I'll swim with you." He offered her his hand.

When they reached the raft, the four of them lay down on their backs with their arms cradling their heads like a pillow. Sarah shivered from the cool night air, but the bright stars in the black sky provided a sense of warmth. The only sound she could hear was the gentle lapping of the waves against the wooden raft.

"Did you make a wish?" asked a friendly voice behind her, drawing her from her memories back to the present.

Sarah turned and saw Hugo standing at the bottom of the steps with a flashlight in hand. He looked handsome in a pair of slim jeans and a textured, beige wool crewneck sweater.

"Hugo, hi." Her voice quivered. "You saw it, too?"

"Yes, do you mind if I sit with you?"

Sarah smiled and patted the space next to her. Hugo took off his black Converse running shoes and placed his gray cabin socks inside. He rolled his jeans into capris and sat down next to Sarah. He turned off his flashlight.

"Ah! The water is cold!" he said as he placed his bare feet into the lake.

Sarah giggled. She studied Hugo's profile in the dark. His nose was slightly crooked, probably the result of a hockey injury, but it just made him that much more handsome.

"Are you having a good time tonight?" she asked.

"Yes, but the women are all over me. I needed some quiet."

"So, Jeff wasn't lying when he said the women find your accent irresistible."

"Just my accent?" Hugo raised his eyebrows and nudged her shoulder with his arm.

Sarah looked down at her feet. Hugo was cocky, but not in an arrogant way. He just seemed to have an accurate view of himself.

"This place reminds me of the lake near my home, without the mountains of course." Hugo sighed. "Svitzerland is so beautiful."

"Are you homesick?"

"Yes. I miss my mother's cooking. She makes the best rosti."

"What's that?"

"It's a Swiss potato dish, like a hash brown or a crispy potato pancake. My mother grates the potatoes and puts them into a frying pan with butter and seasoning salt. After she flips the rosti, she melts cheese on top." Hugo mimicked sprinkling cheese on top of his palm. "The Swiss are known for their cheese, you know."

"That sounds delicious." Sarah's empty stomach growled softly. "Did you grow up playing hockey in Switzerland?"

"My father had me on skates when I was two years old. He believes I can be the next Mark Streit."

"Who is that?"

"He's the greatest up and coming Swiss hockey player!"

Sarah admired his enthusiasm. She pulled her feet out of the lake and wrapped her thin cardigan around herself a little tighter.

"Are you cold?" Hugo pulled off his wool sweater, giving Sarah a glimpse of his well-defined abs before he pulled his t-shirt back down. "Put this on."

Sarah slipped his warm sweater over her head. It smelled woodsy, like the campfire.

"Jeff told me you two are just friends?" he asked.

"Best friends. We've spent every summer together since we were babies."

"Good to know." He winked.

Sarah smiled and placed her chin on her knees. She couldn't tell if he was flirting with her or just being nice. Either way, she was surprised to find herself enjoying the attention. Sarah could feel Hugo was about to put his arm around her shoulders when, suddenly, he stopped.

"Did you hear that?" he asked.

They both listened. Moments later, they heard it again. Someone was retching behind the big tree at the top of the stairs.

"Gross," Sarah said.

The sound of someone puking had ruined their sweet moment and made Sarah feel queasy. Hugo leapt to his feet and held out his hand to Sarah. She accepted his offer and followed him to the bottom of the stairs.

"Hey! Are you okay?" he called up to the wasted party-goer.

An inebriated girl stumbled out from behind the tree and held on to the railing at the top of the stairs for balance. Sarah stared in disbelief and curled her fingers into a fist. "Mabel!" Sarah marched up the stairs and looped her arm through Mabel's.

"I don't," Mabel hiccupped, "feel so good."

When Sarah saw a splatter of fresh vomit on her sister's t-shirt, her anger melted into a puddle of sympathy. "Come on, let's get you home."

"I'm sorry, Sarah," Mabel cried. "I just didn't want to feel sad anymore. I'm so ridicu-lush."

"Anything I can do to help?" Hugo said. He jogged up the stairs and slipped his arm around Mabel's free one.

"Oh, hello, you," Mabel said as her drunk, sleepy eyes began to close. She dropped her sweaty head against Hugo's shoulder.

"I need to get her home, but I don't want to embarrass her," said Sarah. "If we take this trail through the woods, we can avoid parading her through the party."

"You lead the way," said Hugo. He handed Sarah his flashlight and swung Mabel into a newlywed carry, as if he were a groom carrying his bride over the threshold.

Dry sticks cracked beneath their feet as they made their way back to the cottage. Something big rustled in the bushes. Sarah held her breath and flashed the light into the green shrub to see that it was only a tiny brown shrew. She exhaled and continued to lead Hugo through the woods. Sarah had always been afraid of the forest at night.

"We're going to play capture the flag," Jeff had said one summer night when Sarah was twelve. "The goal of the game is for each team to capture the other team's flag and take it back to their zone."

"No way," said Sarah.

"Don't be a baby," said Mabel. "If you don't play, we won't have enough people."

"Not going to happen." Sarah crossed her arms. She was terrified she would be tagged in the opposing team's zone and be forced to sit in the forest jail alone until a teammate could come rescue her.

"Sarah, you can be on my team," suggested Scott. "We will stick together the whole time. I promise."

Sarah relented. The kids marked out their zones, hid their flags, and came up with different strategies to try to capture the other team's flag. Scott led Sarah into the enemy's territory.

"I think I know where they hid it," he whispered.

They slowly wove their way through the trees, but stopped abruptly when they heard a stick crack nearby.

"Sarah, get down!"

They quickly crouched behind a fallen tree and listened as the footsteps got closer and closer. Scott took Sarah's hand in his. She felt safe and warm all over. It was the first time she felt that happy tickle inside her chest.

"Gotcha!" Jeff said as he pounced on them like two sitting ducks.

Sarah gave her head a shake, pushing her childhood memories aside to focus on the task at hand. They had reached the cottage deck. She slowly slid the glass door open and placed a finger to her lips to warn Hugo. She didn't want to wake her mother. Sarah led Hugo into Mabel's bedroom. He gently placed her onto her bed and tiptoed out of the room. Sarah helped Mabel slip out of her jeans and put on a fresh t-shirt for bed. Sarah left the room to grab a warm washcloth, and when she returned, Mabel was curled up in the fetal position.

Sarah knelt by her head and gently washed her face. Before she left, she placed a garbage pail beside her bed and a glass of water on her nightstand. Back in the living area, Sarah could see Hugo at the picnic table outside. She turned on the patio light for him and opened the sliding glass door.

"You're still here?" she whispered. "You should have gone back to the party."

"I wanted to make sure your sister was okay."

"Aside from the killer headache she's bound to wake up with tomorrow, she's fine. Thanks for your help, Hugo."

"Listen, Sarah, I'd like to see you again. Would you want to go out together sometime?"

Sarah thought about Scott and how he had called her his "kid brother's best friend" at the bonfire.

He'll never see me as anything more.

She looked into Hugo's friendly eyes. They were a deep berry blue, like the wild ones she used to pick as a child. "Yes, I'd like that."

Chapter Four

"She's here!" said Sarah.

She watched as Julie's green '80 Toyota Corolla sputtered its way up the steep gravel hill. Sarah's mom worried the old tin can wouldn't make it, but much to everyone's relief, Julie gracefully glided her clunker into the Williams' driveway. Julie stepped out of her car and embraced Sarah.

"I'm so glad to see you!" said Sarah.

"Me, too!"

Sarah helped Julie carry her suitcase, pillow, and guitar into the cottage. They headed straight for the back bedroom and shut the door. Julie flopped onto the bed. "This place always reminds me of the cottages that are featured in those magazines, like *Cottage Life*." She rolled onto her side and propped herself up on an elbow. "It's so beautiful here."

Julie had only been to the cottage a handful of times. She spent most of her summers away at performing arts camps. She dreamed of becoming an actress and singer in Hollywood one day. Sarah believed Julie would make it big. Julie was not only talented, but beautiful, too. Her brown pixie cut made her cheekbones pop on her heart-shaped face. Her short hairstyle automatically brought your attention to her stunning hazel eyes. Even though she measured all of five foot two inches tall, she was feisty and self-assured. Best of all, she was a loyal and loving friend to Sarah.

"I met a guy," said Sarah, "and he's gorgeous."

"Spill. I want to hear every single detail."

Sarah sat down on the bed and filled Julie in on what happened the night of the bonfire.

"You little devil!" said Julie. She smacked Sarah

over the head with her pillow. "I didn't think you had it in you."

"Hey!" said Sarah. She whipped the pillow back in Julie's direction. "He must have changed his mind, though. It's been three days, and I still haven't heard from him."

"Haven't you ever heard of the three-day dating rule?"

Sarah shook her head.

"The rule is a person has to wait three full days before contacting a potential suitor. One day seems too eager, two days is too planned, but three days is, somehow, the perfect amount of time."

"Which means, I should hear from him at some point today..." Sarah's stomach churned.

"How's Jeffrey doing?"

"You know he hates it when you call him that."

"I think the last time I saw him we were fifteen. He was obnoxious, loud, and in desperate need of braces."

"Jeff is still loud and sometimes obnoxious, but he has a nice, straight smile now, thanks to the orthodontist."

"Remember when we invited him to go skinny dipping?"

"I remember when you invited him to go skinny dipping."

****

The girls were fifteen. Julie had a break between musical theatre camp and dance camp, so she'd come to the cottage for a week with the Williams family. The girls had blossomed into young women that summer, and they knew it. They spent hours getting dolled up, as if they were supermodels, to do photoshoots with a disposable camera. They posed sweetly in their light cotton dresses in nearby farmers' fields and took sexier photos in their bikinis down by the dock.

"What are you guys doing?" Jeff said. He paddled his blue kayak past the Williams' dock one evening.

"Wouldn't you like to know," Julie teased. She lay down on the dock and arched her back seductively. Jeff stopped paddling.

Sarah put the camera down and quickly wrapped a towel around her body. Julie waited patiently in her pose, basking in the attention from Jeff, as Sarah picked up the camera again and took the last shot.

"What are you guys doing tonight?" Jeff asked.

"We're going skinny dipping," said Julie.

"No!" said Sarah. "Julie, what?"

"Shh, Sarah," said Julie through gritted teeth.

"Oh, yeah?" he asked.

"After sunset. 9:00 sharp," said Julie.

Suddenly, they heard a loud scratching sound. Jeff, distracted by Julie, had let his kayak float into shallow water. It had glided over a rock and was now stuck. The girls burst into laughter as Jeff tumbled out of his kayak and worked to free his beached boat.

Julie got up and grabbed her towel. As Jeff continued to struggle, Sarah and Julie tiptoed away toward the stairs.

"See you later, Jeffrey!" Julie called as they ran up the steps to the cottage in a fit of giggles.

At 9:00 sharp that night, the girls sat at the edge of the Williams' dock. A half hour passed, but Jeff never showed up. Sarah breathed a sigh of relief.

"His loss," Julie said. She stood up and took off her bikini top.

"What are you doing?" Sarah said.

"What does it look like?" Julie stripped off her bikini briefs and slipped into the lake. "Come on, Sarah, the water is warm."

Hesitant, but curious, Sarah looked around to make sure they were truly alone. Under the cover of darkness, Sarah slowly took off her swimsuit and jumped gleefully into the blackened lake. The water caressed Sarah's bare skin like a silky embrace, and an exhilarating thrill rushed through her body.

****

"I bet Jeff never showed because we were as flat as pancakes back then," said Julie.

"Speak for yourself," said Sarah. They both knew that Sarah with her natural curves had never had a problem filling out her bikini top. "Jeff is a gentleman, that's all. Promise me you'll be nice to him this week?"

"Girls!" Mom called from outside. "Lunch is ready."

"Great, I'm famished," said Julie. She bounced off the bed.

Mom had laid out a white linen tablecloth over the picnic table and placed a milk-colored porcelain vase full of daisies in the center. Mabel, with a miserable expression on her face, sat at the end. Small triangle tea sandwiches of a tasteful variety were arranged neatly on a tray. A full pitcher of lemonade sat beside a platter of homemade chocolate chip cookies, Grandma's special recipe.

"A luncheon to welcome you to Pine Lake," said Mom. She raised a glass of lemonade in Julie's direction.

Mabel moaned and pulled her hoodie over her head.

"I feel like Queen Elizabeth," said Julie. "Thank you, Mrs. Williams. This is wonderful." She filled her plate with crustless cucumber and cream cheese sandwiches. "I'm so hungry."

"It's the fresh air. The food always tastes better

alfresco," said Sarah. She bit into a soft, creamy egg salad sandwich. It tasted like heaven on white bread.

Mabel sat silently at the end of the table and picked at the food on her plate. "I feel so sick," she whined.

"Eat something, Mabel. It will make you feel better," said Mom.

"Don't worry, Mom. It's just a three-day hangover," said Sarah. She glared at her sister as she stuffed the rest of the sandwich in her mouth. She was growing tired of her sister's bad attitude.

"I'm never drinking again," cried Mabel.

Mom stood up and reached her hand across the table to feel Mabel's forehead. "You're burning up! This has gone on long enough. I'm taking you to the walk-in-clinic in town. Go get changed."

Mabel begrudgingly stood from the table and dragged her feet inside the cottage.

"I'm sorry to cut your lunch short," said Mom. She kissed Julie on the crown of her head. "We're so happy you're here. Please make yourself at home. We should be back in time for dinner."

After lunch, Sarah and Julie were drying the last of the dishes by hand when they heard a knock at the sliding back door. Sarah waved for Jeff to come inside.

"Oh, hey, Julie," he said as he slid the door shut behind him. "Sarah told me you were coming today. Hugo and I thought it might be fun to take you two on a tour of the lake on my dad's boat. I packed a picnic with some drinks and snacks."

"Hell, yeah!" said Julie.

Jeff left to go get the boat ready while the girls scrambled to get ready for their date. Sarah settled on a black and white stripe off-the-shoulder bandeau bikini top with black bottoms. She wore her jean short cut-offs over top and slipped her feet into a pair of black platform flip-flops. Julie opted for her bright yellow string bikini and a white crochet cover-up. Sarah stuffed a couple of beach towels into a woven straw tote bag, and they hurried over to the Roberts' dock.

They found Jeff standing in the middle of the boat. "Welcome, ladies! I will be your skipper today on the world-famous Pine Lake boat cruise."

Sarah rolled her eyes and passed Jeff her tote bag. She climbed aboard Mr. Roberts' large pontoon boat with Julie in tow. Hugo was seated on a bench chaise lounge that wrapped around the front of the boat. He smiled at Sarah. "Hey! Come sit with me. The sunshine feels amazing." Hugo placed his Ray-Bans over his eyes and looked up to the sky.

Sarah swallowed and looked over at Julie.

"Go on," said Julie. "I'll be fine. The skipper here is going to teach me how to drive this ship."

Julie winked at Sarah and skipped over to the captain's chair and sat down. Jeff's eyes widened. "Sh-sh—sure, I can teach you," he stammered. Jeff stood behind Julie and wrapped his arms around her to show her how to attach the lanyard and turn on the ignition. Sarah untied the boat from the metal cleats on the dock. Jeff jogged to the back of the boat to double-check that the motor was in the water. When he gave Julie the thumbs up, she placed the throttle lever into drive and slowly guided the pontoon away from the dock and into the bay.

"Woot! That a girl!" Jeff called from the back of the boat.

Sarah slowly walked toward Hugo, but stumbled into his lap when Julie picked up some speed.

"Yahoo!" Julie laughed from the captain's chair.

"Sorry," Sarah said. She climbed off Hugo

awkwardly and sat in her own seat along the bench. She glared at Julie as she struggled to tame her long brown hair that was whipping around wildly in the wind.

"I didn't mind," Hugo said loudly. He wrapped his arm around Sarah's stiff shoulders. She took a deep breath and settled into his chest. He smelled tropical, like coconut and banana sunscreen. The motor was loud and made it difficult to hear anything, so they sat in silence as the boat traveled through the crystal green water. Sarah admired the familiar tall pine trees and moss-covered rock formations that lined the perimeter of the lake. She watched her two best friends from afar and smiled. She couldn't hear what they were saying, but she could tell from their body language that they were becoming wonderfully comfortable in each other's company.

The boat glided toward a tiny island that looked like a painting by an artist in the Group of Seven. Sarah had studied the group of Canadian landscape painters in her high school art history class. Similar to the painting, this island had a lonely jack pine growing out of its rocky earth. Jeff showed Julie how to bring the boat to a stop and drop the anchor.

"These are the rocks I was telling you about," Jeff said to Hugo.

When they were kids, Sarah and Jeff had discovered the island on a canoe trip around the lake. They had stopped on the island to explore and eat the peanut butter and banana sandwiches that Sarah's grandma had packed for them. At the western point of the island, they'd found a rock that looked like a diving board. Jeff had grabbed his snorkel and dove underwater to scout the landing area below.

"It drops off right away," he'd said when he came back up for air. "It's deep."

To the right of the diving rock, there was a

submerged flat rock that was on the perfect incline to act like an underwater staircase. It made it easier for them to climb out of the lake. This spot had quickly become their favorite place to swim. Now, Sarah was excited to introduce this special place to Hugo, and it seemed Jeff was just as excited to show Julie.

"Let's go!" said Hugo.

Sarah kicked off her flip-flops and threw her jean shorts on the bench. The sun was hot and Sarah's olive skin soaked up its rays like a sponge. It was only the beginning of summer, but she already had a golden tan. Hugo reached for her hand, and they plunged into the lake together. The cool water soothed her sun-kissed cheeks. There was something about swimming in the lake that made Sarah feel very much alive. Hugo's playfulness increased his sexiness. Sarah felt an irresistible pull toward him as they kicked their way up to the surface.

"The water feels great," Hugo said when they reached the top. He treaded water with his strong legs and shook his shaggy wet hair like a dog in Sarah's direction.

"Stop it, you mutt," said Sarah. She laughed as she wiped the spray from her face and splashed him back.

"You're cute when you're mad," he said, dodging out of the way.

Sarah dolphin-dived back into the lake and boldly surfaced right in front of him so that they were nose to nose.

"You're beautiful," he said, looking into her eyes.

Sarah blushed. She enjoyed being admired and was attracted to his confidence. They were so close she could feel his warm breath on her lips. She closed her eyes as she felt him inch closer. Suddenly, they heard an earth-shattering scream. Hugo pulled away, and Sarah's eyes snapped open.

"Don't you dare, Jeffrey!" He had thrown Julie

over his shoulder like a sack of potatoes, and she was pounding on his back with her fists. "Let me go!"

"On the count of three. One, two, three!" Jeff stood as straight as a pencil and jumped feet first off the boat with Julie over his shoulder.

Much to Sarah's relief, they surfaced in a fit of giggles.

"I hate you," Julie said. Then, unexpectedly, she swam right up to Jeff, put her arms around his neck, and kissed him.

Sarah shifted her glance away from them. The moment felt private. She slowly relaxed her body into the water as if she were lying down on a bed. She floated on her back and watched the white, fluffy clouds that looked like giant cotton balls drift by. When she was younger, she would often cloud-watch with Scott. They'd strap on their orange lifejackets, swim out into the middle of the bay, and float on their backs while creating a whole new world in the sky from the shapes they could see in the clouds.

"There! Right there! I see a fire-breathing dragon!" Scott would point out.

"I see it! I see it!" said Sarah.

The memory washed away with the waves. Sarah felt Hugo's arm floating beside hers. Her body tensed and her legs began to sink.

"I'm not very good at floating on my back," said Hugo as he struggled to keep his hard body buoyant.

"Look!" Sarah said. "I can see a turtle in the clouds." She pointed to the giant turtle flying across the sky.

"Huh? Where?"

"Right there."

Hugo cocked his head to the right and squinted his eyes.

"Hm. I don't see it."

Sarah felt disappointed, but she pushed those feelings aside. It was a silly game anyway. Hugo tried to bring his legs higher in the water.

"I just keep sinking."

"That's because you're all muscle."

Hugo reached for her hand. His fingers laced through hers and their palms pressed together. It was the sweet beginning of something new.

It was almost dinner time when Sarah and Julie got back to the cottage. They were ravenous after having spent the entire afternoon out on the water. Mom and Mabel were home from the clinic.

"Oh, you're back! Go get changed. I picked us up a wood oven pizza for dinner," said Mom.

"It smells amazing, Mrs. Williams."

"What's the doctor's cure for your hangover?" Sarah asked Mabel.

"It's strep throat, you jerk."

"That's enough, you two," said Mom. "Sarah, can you plate the pizza? I'm going to whip together a quick salad, but I need to call your father. There was an issue with the health insurance at the pharmacy. I had to pay for Mabel's antibiotics in full."

Julie excused herself to change into some dry clothes. Mom picked up the phone and placed it on speaker in order to slice the cucumber. Dad's secretary answered on the first ring.

"Jack Williams' office, Bridget speaking."

"Hi Bridget, it's Alice. Is Jack available?"

"Oh, hi, Mrs. Williams. I'm sorry, he's in a meeting right now. Is there something I can help you with?"

"Yes, our daughter is sick, and I tried to use our health insurance to pay for her antibiotics at the pharmacy today, and it was rejected."

"Oh, well the waiting period must be over. Jack's new British Columbia health insurance must have kicked in."

"Waiting period?"

"Yes, when someone moves permanently from one province to another, they are subjected to a waiting period before their new benefits begin."

"Moved permanently?" Mabel mouthed to Sarah.

Sarah shrugged. His secretary must be mistaken. Dad had only signed a six-month contract. Sarah looked to her mother. There was something about the expression on Mom's face that made Sarah feel as though someone had kicked her in the gut with a steel toed boot.

"Is there anything else I can help you with Mrs. Williams?"

"No, thank you, Bridget. You've been a tremendous help."

ALYSSA DELLE PALME

Chapter Five

A storm was brewing. Sarah could sense it. She woke up at the crack of dawn having tossed and turned all night. She couldn't stop thinking about what Bridget had said, and Mom didn't want to talk about it. When Sarah saw a sliver of pink sky on the horizon, she got dressed and went to the kitchen to start breakfast.

Pink sky in the morning, sailors warning, she thought.

Moments later, her mother emerged from her bedroom. She was dressed to take Pete for a run. "Come with us," she said.

It was only 5:00, but Sarah could already feel her hair sticking to the back of her neck. The humid air smelled sweet, and the treetops were still.

The calm before the storm.

Pete trotted alongside them as they picked up their pace. Mom always said running helped her get her thoughts in order. The arches of Sarah's feet ached as they pounded against the dirt road. Her lungs burned and her legs screamed at her to stop, but she kept pace with her mother. They ran until they reached the century-old stone church and cemetery, where they finally stopped so they could catch their breath.

When Sarah and Mabel were little girls, Mom and Dad would often take them for a walk after dinner to tire them out for bedtime. The church was their turnaround spot.

"Your father once said he thought we should be buried here after we die. That way, you and Mabel could visit our graves when you come up to the cottage in the summer."

"Mom, that's morbid."

Mom nodded. "I prefer to picture us growing old and gray together." Her brow creased with worry.

"Is everything all right, Mom? Is this about the health insurance?"

"I just can't fathom why your father would keep something like this from me. There has to be an explanation. He can't just up and move across the country permanently without telling me."

"Why don't you just call him back and—"

"No, I'm sure Bridget was mistaken. I'll wait until he's here to talk to him."

Lightning flashed in the distance. Pete whined at their feet. The treetops began to sway in the wind, like old friends waving hello. Sarah counted Mississippis until she heard the thunder. "The storm is still six kilometers away. We have enough time to make it back."

Thunder boomed overhead as they reached the cottage. Sarah took off Pete's leash, and he scurried inside. When they walked through the front door, they were greeted with the comforting smells of sizzling bacon and hot coffee. Sarah took her seat at the breakfast table and filled her mug to the brim with the warm black brew.

"Good morning," said Mabel. She kissed Mom on her flushed cheek and flipped a pancake onto her plate. "Did you two go for a run?"

"We did," said Mom. "You must be feeling better."

Mabel added more pancake mix to the griddle. "Much better. The antibiotics are doing their thing."

Mom cut a piece of her pancake, dipped it into the amber maple syrup, and put the fluffy flapjack in her mouth. "These are delicious, Mabel."

"Grandma's recipe."

"Mm. I forgot how hungry running makes you. Please pass the bacon."

Sarah and Mabel stared at their mother with wide eyes.

"Really? But you said bacon was as unhealthy as smoking cigarettes," said Sarah.

"One piece won't kill me."

Sarah offered her the plate, and Mom took a dripping piece of bacon off the grease-soaked paper towel. Sarah took a piece for herself and bit into the chewy red ribbon of fat. She closed her eyes, savoring its salty taste. She took another sip of hot coffee to wash down the bacon bits. "Where's Julie?"

"Still asleep," said Mabel. She plated the last of the pancakes and unplugged the griddle. "I have to go jump in the shower. My first shift at the restaurant starts at 9:00."

"I'll drive you," Mom called out as Mabel left the kitchen. She turned her attention back to Sarah. "It was nice to have you all to myself this morning. I've barely seen you this week."

Sarah scooped a spoonful of steaming scrambled eggs onto her plate. "Julie and I have just been making the most of our time together."

"With Jeff and Hugo, I hear."

Sarah rolled her eyes. "Yes, with Jeff and Hugo, too. We're all going to canoe to the big island tomorrow and camp out for a night."

"You're being safe?"

Sarah felt a deep blush rise. She fidgeted with her napkin. She knew what her mother was asking, but she didn't feel like explaining to her that she was still a virgin.

"Not that it's any of your business, but Hugo and I are just getting to know each other."

"And Julie?" whispered Mom. She looked over her shoulder at the back bedroom. "Is she on the pill?"

"Mom!"

"Okay, okay." Mom raised her hands in surrender. "So, tell me about Hugo. What's he like?"

"Well, as you already know, he's extremely good-looking." Sarah smiled at her mother. "He knows it, too. I find him interesting, and he's incredibly sweet." Sarah took a bite of her eggs and looked out the window. "It looks like the storm is passing."

The rain had slowed to a gentle rhythm on the roof. The low, dark clouds that had gathered and loomed overhead earlier were now dispersing.

"I'm going to drive back to the city for a night," said Mom. "I need to pick up the mail and check on the house. Do you need anything for your camping trip?"

"No, we're all set to go."

After the dishes were done, Sarah sat at the kitchen table all morning, furiously writing in her spiral notebook. The run had inspired her, and it felt as though the fresh air had magnified her creativity. It was noon by the time Julie got out of bed.

"I'm following the smell of bacon to its source," Julie murmured as she entered the kitchen. Her nightgown, an oversize Tragically Hip t-shirt, fell just above her knees, a souvenir from a concert in Kingston. She sported impressive bedhead. "Good morning." Julie yawned.

"More like 'good afternoon.'" Sarah put down her pencil. "I saved you a plate. You can reheat it in the oven."

"What are you working on?"

Sarah stared at the jumble of words in her notebook. She didn't know yet. She was still trying to find her voice. "Our camping list," she lied.

Sarah and Julie spent the rest of their day packing for the canoe trip. They planned and prepared their meals ahead of time. Homemade granola with nuts, dried cranberries, cinnamon, and honey was on the menu for their breakfast. For dinner, they made a pot of spicy chili with peppers and sweet potatoes. Sarah added croissants, cheese, deli meat, and a bottle of mustard into the cooler. They would make sandwiches for lunch. Sarah put new batteries in their headlamps and placed their sleeping bags and pillows into black garbage bags to protect them from getting wet. She checked her list twice.

"We're ready," Sarah said.

Early the next morning, when the water was calm and the sunshine peeked out from behind the horizon of pine trees, Sarah and Julie packed their gear into the Williams' green canoe. From the dock, they could see Jeff and Hugo were busy hauling their own camping equipment into the Roberts' canoe. Sarah and Julie loaded the heavier items, like the cooler, tent, and water in the center of the boat. The lighter items like pillows and sleeping bags were jammed into the bow and stern. By the time they were done packing their canoe, it was as stuffed as Italian cannelloni.

Sarah squeezed into the rear of the boat while Julie sat up front. It took a moment for them to find their stride, but soon they were paddling with ease to the Roberts' dock. Jeff and Hugo were ready and patiently waiting for them in their red canoe. The guys paddled out to create their convoy. The lake was still, and the canoes sliced through the water like a blue heron's sharp bill hunting for fish. The gentle breeze carried a sap-sweet smell from the pine trees that surrounded them. Sarah and Julie fell into the comfortable silence of two sisters. A loon announced its presence at the mouth of the bay. Its haunting call seemed to wish them farewell as they headed off on their adventure.

The islands in Pine Lake belonged to the Crown,

and camping was only permitted on one, Dead Fish Island. Sarah and Mabel had discovered the small island when they were kids while on a canoe trip with their parents. Mom and Dad had let the girls out of the canoe to explore the islet while they spread out a picnic lunch. While they played explorers, Sarah found a dead fish in the sand. Mabel proceeded to plant a flag in the dirt, which she had made using a stick and a brown leaf, then declared the newfound land Dead Fish Island. The name stuck.

Once the couples arrived at their site, they worked together to unload the canoes and set up camp. Sarah showed Julie how to raise the tent and stake it to the ground. Meanwhile, Jeff used straps to hang a hammock between two large trees. Hugo collected fallen sticks and dry bark to use for kindling. By lunch time, they all collapsed into their camping chairs and dug into the croissant sandwiches Sarah had prepared. Hugo reached for Sarah's hand and kissed it.

"This sandwich is delicious. Thank you."

Sarah was drawn to the melody of his accent and the fullness of his bottom lip. She imagined what it would feel like to press her lips against his. Hugo had a way of making her feel like the most beautiful woman he had ever laid eyes on, even when she was wearing her camel-colored hiking pants.

"To the chef," said Jeff. He raised a can of beer in Sarah's direction.

It was the perfect summer day. There wasn't a cloud in the sky, and the glinting sun was so powerful the couples could jump into the cool water with ease. When they needed a break from the sun, they found refuge under the canopy of trees. The shade was nature's air conditioning. They spent most of the afternoon in the water. Sarah and Hugo snorkeled around the island hand in hand. The lake floor was a diverse landscape of green seaweed, rocks, and snail shells.

When Sarah was a preteen, she spent most of her summer reading, working on her tan, and snorkeling with Scott. Together, they invented their own sign language to communicate underwater.

"When I do this," Scott had said, showing her a fist with one hand and a peace sign with the other, "that means school of fish."

Sarah enjoyed another snorkeling game they used to play even more. They would keep their masks on but remove their mouthpieces. One person would shout something under water and the other person had to guess what they were trying to say.

"I love you!" Sarah had shouted at Scott underwater. Big air bubbles floated out of her mouth and up to the surface as she professed her feelings.

"You want lunch?" Scott had guessed.

A school of minnows suddenly appeared on Sarah's left-hand side, bringing her back to reality. She held her breath and watched the tiny, silver fish swimming in sync. She pulled her hand away from Hugo to sign "school of fish," but immediately remembered that only Scott understood the secret language. Instead, she pointed toward the group. Hugo's eyes widened before he moved toward them too quickly, scaring them away.

When their fingers wrinkled like raisins, Sarah and Hugo emerged from the lake and laid face down on their beach towels in the sand. It was hot enough to air-dry. Their wet backs broiled under the sun. Hugo sat up and reached for his sunscreen, offering to put some on Sarah's back. She nodded. He casually untied her bikini top from around her neck and slowly massaged the cool, white cream onto her shoulder blades.

"That feels good," she murmured into her arms.

Sarah was surprised at how sexy she felt around Hugo, like a grown woman. She could feel him adoring every inch of her body as he rubbed the sunscreen into her skin. Hugo retied her bikini top and gently rolled Sarah onto her back. He straddled her in the sand and pinned her hands above her head. Her breath quickened, and she licked her lips. The weight of his body on her pelvis sent warm tingles throughout the rest of her body.

"You're so beautiful," he said. He leaned down and pressed his full lips against hers. Sarah took her time as she gently explored his mouth with hers. She sucked on his plump bottom lip, relishing in the adrenaline rush of their first kiss.

"Yeah, buddy!" Jeff shouted from the lake. He and Julie whooped and hollered as they ran out of the water and plopped themselves in the sand right next to Sarah and Hugo. Sarah covered her face with her hands as Hugo moved back onto his own towel.

"Hugo and Sarah, sitting in a tree..." Jeff sang.

"Shut up," Sarah mumbled.

"You don't have to be embarrassed," said Julie. She pried Sarah's hands away from her face. "That was quite some kiss, though. Wow."

"Took you guys long enough," said Jeff. "I was beginning to wonder if Sarah had put you in the friend zone." He patted Hugo, who was grinning ear to ear, on the back.

Sarah and Hugo spent the rest of the day stealing kisses. It simply felt good. Still, every time Hugo pulled away, Sarah couldn't help but wonder what it would feel like to kiss Scott. Would his lips be as soft and warm as Hugo's? These thoughts frustrated her. Scott wasn't interested, but Hugo, who was both good-looking and sweet, was totally into her. To distract herself from further thoughts of Scott, Sarah began to prepare their dinner over the campfire. It wasn't long before Hugo approached her from behind and softly kissed the nape of her neck. Sarah paused, imagining just for a moment, that it was Scott.

"I find this particular curve of your body irresistible," Hugo whispered. He gently caressed her neck, sending shivers down her spine. Determined to push all thoughts of Scott away, Sarah leaned back and surrendered into Hugo. Her heart might not be up to speed for this, but her body most certainly was. Hugo knew how to make her feel good.

"Watching you react to my touch is a major turn-on," he said.

Later, as the couples made s'mores for dessert, Sarah noticed that Hugo had a piece of fluffy marshmallow stuck to his bottom lip. She leaned over and kissed him, tracing the tip of her tongue along his mouth. The sweet taste of marshmallow still lingered on his lips.

As the sun began to set, Sarah and Hugo laid an unzipped sleeping bag inside the hammock and crawled in. Sarah snuggled into Hugo's firm chest, and they watched the night sky light up one star at a time from the comfort of their swaying bed. Despite being cuddled in the hammock like a sleepy caterpillar in its cocoon, Sarah could still feel the cool breeze on her exposed skin. She didn't know if it was the night air or being so close to Hugo that gave her goosebumps.

"Today was the best day," said Hugo. He laced his fingers through hers and kissed the back of her hand. "I have a feeling we're going to have an awesome summer."

Sarah's heart thumped in her chest. She no longer wanted to stonewall the new feelings that stirred up inside her whenever Hugo was around just because she found them confusing. She wanted to put herself out there.

"I like you, Hugo." She held her breath as she waited for his response. Her legs twitched uncomfortably in the sleeping bag, and seconds felt like hours.

"What's not to like?" Hugo winked at Sarah, and she poked him in the ribs a few times with her index fingers. "Okay, okay! I like you, too! Enough with the tickle torture."

Sarah had meant to sleep in the tent with Julie that night, but the symphony of crickets, the warmth of Hugo's body, and the gentle swing of the hammock rocked Sarah's tired body into a deep, comfortable sleep.

The next morning, the romantic hues and soft radiance of last night's sunset was replaced with a thick blanket of dull, gray clouds. Sarah dragged her feet as she took down the tent with Julie.

"Tired from last night?" Julie asked. She looked over her shoulder to see where the guys were and lowered her voice. "Did you guys sleep together? You never made it back to the tent."

"Yes, we slept together," Sarah whispered. "But we didn't have sex if that's what you're asking."

Julie bent down and pulled a stake out of the ground. Sarah crossed her arms and tapped her foot. "Spill. Did you and Jeff sleep together?"

"For your information, yes, we did sleep in the tent together … in separate sleeping bags."

"Do you like him?" Sarah asked.

"I do. I really like him." Julie lowered her voice. "I think he has the potential to be the one I lose my V-card to."

Sarah raised her eyebrows.

"You look surprised," said Julie.

"You've loathed Jeff for as long as I can

remember."

Julie shrugged. "He's different now. More mature, I guess. He's incredibly sweet, too."

Sarah smiled. Julie was smitten. She liked seeing her best friends happy. They were a good match.

"I better be maid of honor at your wedding," Sarah said.

"Oh, shut up!" Julie playfully smacked Sarah on the arm.

Sarah removed a pole from the body of the tent, folded it up, and placed it in the bag. "Didn't you think yesterday was the most incredible day? I don't want our camping trip to end. And I hate that you're going back to the city."

"Aw, Sarah." Julie dropped her tent pole and wrapped her best friend in a hug. "Don't be upset. I'm coming back at the end of summer, remember?"

Sarah nodded and gave Julie a half smile. The couples worked all morning to break down their campsite. They repacked their canoes with their camping gear, ensured the fire was out, and did one final walk around to make sure they didn't leave a trace.

"The campsite looks cleaner than we found it," said Jeff. He leaned over and kissed Julie goodbye. "I'll call you."

"You'd better."

Hugo held out his hand to help Sarah balance as she climbed into her tippy green canoe. "See you around, beautiful." He kissed her on the cheek and launched the girls' heavy canoe into the lake with one effortless push.

The sky was still overcast, and the water was choppy. Sarah's arms burned as she struggled to paddle against the current. Julie sat calmly up front with her paddle across her lap, taking in the scenery.

"You're going to have to help if you want to make

it back to the cottage!" Sarah called from the stern.

Julie turned toward Sarah and grinned sheepishly. "Busted." Julie dipped her paddle into the lake, and together they began to make headway. An eagle soared above leading them towards the cottage.

Mom and Mabel were eating lunch outside at the picnic table when Sarah and Julie arrived back.

"How was camping? I want to hear all about it," said Mom. "I didn't know what time you would be back, so I didn't make you anything. I could quickly whip something up."

"I'd love to join you, but I need to shower before driving back to the city," said Julie.

"I'm not hungry," said Sarah. "Thanks, though."

"Julie, there are fresh towels on the bed and, Sarah, I left your mail on your bedside table."

The girls dumped their gear on the floor in the living area. While Julie went to shower, Sarah flipped through her mail—a postcard from her dad in B.C., a statement from her bank, and a thin envelope from a provincial arts council. She ripped open the letter, destroying the envelope in the process. She held her breath and skimmed through the letter.

Dear Ms. Williams,

We regret to inform you that you were not selected to receive the award this year. Unfortunately, the Foundation does not have the resources to provide a scholarship to each worthy applicant. We wish you the best in pursuing your education goals.

The letter was signed by a grants and scholarships committee representative. Sarah's heart sank. Without this scholarship, she couldn't afford to go to school.

Chapter Six

Sarah woke up early the next morning. She showered, blow-dried her hair, and slipped on a white cotton summer dress that accentuated her post-beach-day tan. She slid her favorite turquoise mala bead bracelet around her wrist and put on a pair of brown leather flip flops. When she was ready, she took the shortcut through the pine grove to the Roberts' cottage. She found Scott in the driveway, packing his truck for work. He wore dark green swim trunks with a Pine Lake Beach patch sewn onto the bottom corner. On top, he wore a sleeveless dark green shirt that read LIFEGUARD in bright white letters across his chest. His arm muscles flexed as he threw a duffle bag into the back of his truck.

Sarah took a deep breath. "Hey, Scott."

"Oh! Sarah, I didn't see you there. This is a nice surprise." Scott put down his lunch cooler.

"Does your offer to put in a good word for me with your boss still stand?"

"Get in," he said, holding open the passenger side door.

On the drive to the public beach, Sarah filled Scott in. "I didn't get the scholarship. If I don't find a job quickly, I won't be going to Concordia in September."

Scott kept his eyes on the road, but reached over and squeezed Sarah's hand. "I'm sorry about the scholarship."

The warmth of his hand was comforting, like a cozy sweater on a rainy day, and helped to subdue her anxiety.

"A lifeguard just quit, so they're looking to hire. You'd really be doing them a favor."

"Why did they quit?"

"My boss, Kurt, is an asshole. Still want the job?"

Sarah nodded. "I need it."

When they arrived at Pine Lake Beach, Scott brought Sarah to the small, rusty-red lifeguard shack in the sand. One side of the hut housed lifejackets and paddles of all sizes. Beachgoers could rent canoes and kayaks, and it was the lifeguards' responsibility to fit them with an appropriate Personal Floatation Device. The other side of the shack was used as a First Aid station. They found Kurt inside, organizing the first aid kits. Sarah was intimidated by his stature. He was a huge bald guy with a large chest and skinny legs.

"Kurt, I'd like to introduce you to my friend, Sarah. She's interested in the lifeguard position."

Kurt put down his clipboard and looked Sarah up and down. His eyes landed on her chest. "Do you have any … experience?" His tone sounded as if he were asking if she had experience of a different kind. He rubbed his fat fingers through his greasy blond goatee. Sarah shivered.

"She is a certified lifeguard and has worked at her community pool in the city," said Scott.

"Well, beachfront lifeguarding is more challenging," said Kurt. He never took his eyes off Sarah.

"I trained and earned all of my certifications right here at Pine Lake," she said. "I'm familiar with the beach."

"You'd be expected to participate in a one-on-one training session with me to make sure you're at the top of your game."

Sarah cringed. "Yes, I understand."

"When can you start?"

Early the next morning, Sarah met Kurt at the beach for a training session before her first shift. She had arranged to get rides to work with Scott. When they arrived at the beach, Scott set himself up in a chair in the sand with a stack of books he was required to read before school started. Kurt wasn't pleased to see Scott.

"Don't you have a life?" Kurt muttered under his breath. "Come on, chickee, we've got work to do."

For the next hour, Kurt and Sarah practiced different rescue drills in the sand. He showed her various patron surveillance techniques and reviewed her CPR skills.

"You're doing great," he said. He pulled a stopwatch out of his pocket. "Lastly, you need to swim five-hundred meters in ten minutes."

Sarah stripped down to her dark green one-piece bathing suit with the small Pine Lake Beach patch sewn onto the top corner. She grabbed a red rescue torpedo and placed its black strap across her body.

"Girl, you make the uniform look good." Kurt licked his crusty, sunburned lips.

"Thanks," she mumbled.

Sarah walked away from him as quickly as she could and dove into the cold lake. She finished the challenge in under eight minutes.

Kurt stared at Sarah's chest as she got out of the lake. "I can see the water must be cold."

She quickly grabbed her towel and wrapped it around her shoulders, covering her hard nipples. When Kurt walked up behind her and started massaging her shoulders, Sarah's whole body stiffened like the straight orange spinal board that leaned against the lifeguard chair tower.

"Rescues tend to be more frequent for beachfront lifeguards than for those working at pools," he said. He roughly kneaded her upper back with his fat thumbs. "That means there's more action, but it can also be more stressful." Kurt took another step toward Sarah and pressed his entire body against her back. She could feel every inch, and she froze. She was unable to think, move, or even breathe. "You just come to me if you're in need of a little stress release," he whispered in her ear.

"Hey, how did it go?" Scott interrupted. He'd jogged up behind them, books in hand.

Kurt immediately dropped his hands and stepped aside. "She did very well. Isn't that right, chickee?"

Sarah wrapped her towel around her shoulders a little tighter and nodded.

"Well, I better go check the inventory of the first aid kits," said Kurt. He narrowed his eyes at Scott. "You can get started on the washroom. I clogged the toilet this morning."

Sarah glared at Kurt as he walked from the shoreline back to the lifeguard shack. The back of his neck was so fat it folded over the collar of his shirt.

"He's such an asshole," said Scott.

"How do you work for this guy?"

"The job pays well, and I need the money. Everyone else is cool, though." When Scott gently placed his hand on her shoulder, Sarah winced. A concerned look flashed across his face. "Hey, are you okay? Did something happen?"

Sarah didn't know how to answer him. Her brain was searching for a way out of the fog. She kept replaying what had happened and wondered if maybe she had led Kurt on in some way.

It's my fault, she thought. *I shouldn't have stripped down to my bathing suit in front of him.*

Guilt sat on her chest like a heavy brick. She looked at Scott's furrowed brow. There stood her friend who had put his own reputation on the line to get her this job, and here she was almost blowing it on her first day.

"Everything is fine."

Sarah was assigned to shadow another lifeguard

named Shannon for her first shift. Shannon was delighted to have a tag along for the day.

"People, like, always think lifeguarding is, like, such a cool job but, like, it can be, like, totally boring."

Despite speaking like a valley girl, Shannon was smart. She was studying nursing at the University of Ottawa and dreamed of working with premature babies. Sarah was mesmerized by Shannon's long, blonde hair that was so voluminous she could star in one of those shampoo commercials. Shannon spent the day teaching Sarah the ins and outs of the job. They reviewed all the policies and procedures, and then Shannon showed Sarah how the rotation worked.

"We rotate positions, like, every thirty minutes to help keep us, like, focused and alert."

Between counting heads and directing swimmers to stay within the buoys, Shannon filled Sarah in on all the staff gossip.

"So, Kurt is, like, such a loser. He's twenty-five and still lives in his mom's basement. All his friends are away at college or, like, getting married, and he's still partying with junior lifeguards on weekends."

Shannon waved to another lifeguard as they rotated from the tall lifeguard chair tower to the First Aid station in the shack.

"That's my best friend, Britney. She looks like a bitch, but that's just her face."

Sarah watched Britney as she climbed the chair tower with ease and took her position to supervise the water. Shannon was right. Britney's expressionless face did look naturally mean. She also looked like she had stepped off the pages of *Teen Vogue* magazine. She was as tall and slim as a supermodel, but not the calorie-counting kind. She had a tiny waist and a voluptuous chest like a Victoria Secret model. With her long red hair and big boobs, Britney reminded Sarah of Jessica Rabbit but with freckles.

"Britney is like obsessed with Scott," said Shannon. "What's your deal with him anyway?"

"We're good friends."

"By good friends, do you mean like friends with benefits?"

"I mean, we've known each other since we were babies. Our cottages are divided by a small pine grove."

Shannon's eyes bored into Sarah's as if she were trying to determine if Sarah was telling the truth or not. "Well, Britney and Scott hooked up all last summer, but she says he's been acting distant this year."

Sarah shrugged. Shannon's guess was as good as hers.

"Speak of the devil. Here he comes now." Shannon waved.

Scott jogged toward the First Aid station. "How's your first day going?" he asked Sarah.

"Great." Sarah smiled at Scott. "You're sweet for checking in."

A faint twinkle touched the depths of his green eyes. "Of course. Let me know if you need anything."

Shannon raised her perfectly groomed eyebrows. "Shouldn't you be at the boat launch?"

Scott blinked and turned his attention to Shannon. "It's been a busy day for canoe and kayak rentals. Kurt and I need your help."

While Shannon went to the boat launch beside the lake, Sarah spent the rest of her shift fitting kids for lifejackets and paddles in the shack. From the hut, Sarah had a clear view of Scott, who was busy helping families haul their boats from the canoe rack to the water. She admired how his eyes lit up every time he spoke to one of the little kids. She noticed that their mothers found that attractive as well. At the end of the day, she went around the hut with a clipboard to ensure all the lifejackets and paddles had been returned. She was so absorbed by her work she didn't hear Kurt come in.

"Hey, chickee."

Sarah dropped her clipboard, and it clattered against the worn linoleum flooring in the shack.

"Kurt, you scared me."

He smiled. Kurt seemed to get off on making young women feel uncomfortable. He was as unwelcome as a period in white pants. Sarah picked up her clipboard and moved behind a barrel of paddles. She needed to put something between her and Kurt. He was blocking the only exit with his ogre-sized body.

"I was wondering if you wanted to get some dinner with me."

Sarah shuddered. His crooked front teeth that were stained yellow from too much nicotine and caffeine were enough to make her lose her appetite.

"I can't. I'm having dinner with my family tonight."

"What about dessert?" Kurt winked and stepped closer to Sarah.

The tiny, wispy hair on the back of her neck stood up. "I ... I have a boyfriend." Her voice was barely audible, but she was screaming on the inside.

"You know, Sarah, what happens in the shack stays in the shack."

As Kurt was about to take another step toward Sarah, Scott suddenly appeared and pushed passed him.

"Hey, babe," Scott said. He walked around the barrel of paddles and planted a kiss on her cheek. The warmth of his lips thawed her from her frozen state. "Ready to go?"

"Wait, you two are together? I thought you were

just friends."

Scott grabbed Sarah's hand and guided her to the door of the hut. "We've been on a few dates, but I'm sure you can understand that I don't want to get into more details about our personal lives. See you tomorrow, Kurt."

Scott pulled Sarah out the door and led her around the building to the entrance of the staff changeroom. His jaw was clenched. "He didn't touch you, did he?" He put his hands in his pockets and began pacing back and forth. "You know, I've heard rumors about that guy."

Sarah looked at her feet. She worried if she admitted the truth, Scott would act impulsively by beating Kurt to a pulp. While part of her found his knight-in-shining-armor bit attractive, she refused to be the reason why Scott lost his job.

"He just asked me out, Scott. It's really not a big deal."

"It is a big deal. I got you this job and put you in that position." Scott ran both his hands through his mop of curls. "He's such a creep."

Sarah gently placed a hand on his shoulder, which seemed to relax the rigid cords in his neck. "This isn't your fault, Scott. I'm fine, really."

Sarah went inside the changeroom to get out of her uniform while Scott waited outside. She wrapped her damp bathing suit in her towel and slipped into a sky-blue tunic dress with flutter sleeves. She completed the look with a pair of white platform flip-flops. Her outfit was both laidback and polished. Her hair had benefited from a little lake-water texture, so she scrunched her long locks to create natural beachy waves. She twisted a small section of hair back toward her ear and pinned it in place with a sparkly butterfly clip. She applied a clear vanilla flavored Lip Smacker gloss to her lips. When she emerged from the changeroom, Scott's brow relaxed, free of frown lines.

"You clean up nice," he said. Scott wrapped his arm around her shoulders, and they walked toward the parking lot. "I'm sorry if I acted like an ass earlier. Kurt makes my blood boil."

On their way to Scott's truck, they saw Kurt, Shannon, and Britney huddled outside the First Aid station, sharing a cigarette. As soon as they approached, the trio stopped talking. Britney and Shannon glared at Sarah, who suddenly realized that Kurt must have told them that she and Scott were an item. Scott's arm around her shoulders solidified his story. As Scott waved goodbye to their co-workers, Sarah quickly escaped from underneath his arm. Shannon rolled her eyes.

"Liar," Britney coughed into her hand as Sarah passed by.

"What was that about?" Scott asked once they were a safe distance away.

Sarah shrugged. She was already in enough trouble with Shannon and Britney. She didn't want to add to the drama. "Thanks again for today, Scott. You saved me from a very awkward conversation."

Scott's eyes clung to hers. Sarah sensed he was struggling with something. He cleared his throat. "I'm always here for you, Sarah. I…"

Sarah held her breath and waited for him to finish his thought, but it seemed as though he couldn't bring himself to say what he wanted to say.

"I mean, you're Jeff's best friend. It's my job to look out for you," he finished.

Sarah exhaled noisily through her pursed lips like a deflated balloon. That was not the direction she thought the conversation was taking.

What did I expect from the person that has put me

in the friend zone permanently?

Sarah tossed her bag into the back of Scott's truck, climbed into the passenger seat, and silently stewed in her disappointment.

"Is Mabel working at Fiddleheads Pub again this summer?"

Sarah nodded.

"Do you want to go there and grab a bite to eat?"

When Sarah used to fantasize about Scott asking her out to dinner, she had imagined that she would be thrilled at his invitation. However, his offer just made her feel tired and defeated. Sarah held her head high and locked eyes with his. "I can't. I have a date with Hugo."

Chapter Seven

"What's the matter with you?" Mabel asked Sarah. She passed the bowl of salad to Mom and reached for the dressing. Mabel stirred the oil and balsamic vinegar together in the glass dish before drizzling it on top of her salad with the spoon. Mom always put condiments in small bowls, even ketchup. She deemed cans and bottles at the dining table unsightly.

"She worked all day," said Mom, answering for Sarah. "Are you tired, honey?"

"I'm fine," Sarah said. She took a small bite of salmon that her mother had grilled on a cedar plank on the barbeque. The fish was infused with a fresh wood flavor and melted in her mouth. She lifted the tongs to serve herself the fresh spring mix that Mom had bought at the Farmer's Market earlier that day. Sarah's favorite part of the salad was the edible flowers. It was the showpiece of the dinner table.

"Nervous about your date with Hugo?" Mom asked.

Sarah shook her head. She couldn't explain to her mother that the reason she was feeling down was because she preferred to be going on a date with Scott.

"Where's Hugo taking you?" Mabel asked.

"We're going to the fair."

Every year, the town of Thorny Bush hosted the fair over the Canada Day long weekend. It was a mix of agricultural and entertainment events, rides, games, and greasy food trucks. The fairgrounds were only a 15-minute drive from their cottage, but their mother dreaded going. She worried the rides were faulty and there was always a pile of vomit somewhere. She hated the long lines, and the porta-potties were disgusting. Unlike her mother, Sarah looked forward to the fair. When she was younger, her mother stayed behind at the cottage, and her grandma would take her and Mabel to the fair.

"I don't want to wear my hair in a bun!" Eight-year-old Mabel kicked her little legs in protest as her mother tied her hair up.

"Trust me, you don't want your hair getting stuck in a ride," said Mom.

Their mom's anxieties never rubbed off on the girls. To Sarah, the fair was much more than just rides and hot dogs—it was a special day with their grandma. With their hair tied up, dressed in matching red and white dresses, with temporary tattoos of the Canadian flag rubbed onto their cheeks, they'd wave goodbye to their mother as they left for a day of adventure and cotton candy.

Grandma never bought single-ride tickets. She splurged for the ride-all-day bracelets. Sarah's favorite ride was the spinning strawberry. She liked that the ride was propelled from the people sitting inside the strawberry and how she could control how fast or slow the giant metal fruit spun.

"That's a baby ride," said Mabel. She tugged at the hem of their grandmother's shirt. "I want to go on the flying swings, Grandma!"

The girls waited patiently in line, and when it was their turn, the toothless carnival worker helped them into their swings that were suspended from metal chains on a rotating carousel top. Sarah held on for dear life with her little hands. Halfway through the ride, she looked over at her sister, whose face had lost all its color. Moments later, Mabel leaned over her swing and puked. To Sarah, it all happened in slow motion. She watched as the spinning puke pancake made its way around Mabel and splattered all over the little boy behind them. Mabel came off the ride clean as a whistle.

"Please pass the butter," said Mom.

The sound of her mother's voice pulled Sarah back to the dinner table. She handed her mother the butter dish.

"Germs spread like crazy at the fair," said Mom. "Make sure you wash your hands."

"And avoid the flying swings," Mabel suggested.

After dinner, Sarah brushed her teeth, reapplied her clear lip gloss, and went outside when Hugo honked the horn.

"Hey, gorgeous, get in."

It was a warm summer evening, and they drove through the countryside with their windows rolled all the way down. Sarah turned up the volume on the radio when she heard Britney Spears' new song, "Sometimes." Hugo kept both hands on the wheel as he drove on the winding roads through the forest and then up and down the picturesque hills to the flat country highway. Sarah particularly enjoyed this part of the view because she could clearly see the local farmhouses. Sarah often daydreamed what it would be like to live in one of those charming stone houses in the middle of a cornfield.

When they arrived at the fairgrounds, a traffic guard directed Hugo to park in a grassy field. After he turned off the ignition, he leaned into Sarah and gently kissed her glossy lips.

"Mm. You taste like cupcakes. I've been waiting to do that all day," he said.

Pangs of guilt kept Sarah from making eye contact. Here she had this great-looking guy who complimented her and asked her out on dates, but who she hadn't thought about once while she'd been at work with Scott. In that moment, Sarah decided it was finally time to put her crush on Scott behind her. She took Hugo's hands in hers. "Let's go! I can't wait to take you on the Ferris wheel."

Their first date at the fair reminded Sarah of one of those cute dates you see in the movies. After Hugo bought the ride tickets, they walked through the fairgrounds hand in hand, trying to decide what they should do first. They went for a spin on the strawberries before braving the Tilt-A-Whirl and Gravitron. As they stumbled out of the spaceship-shaped ride, they decided it was probably best to take a break and try their luck at the games.

Sarah's favorite carnival game was the water gun race where you competed against other players. The goal was to shoot the water on the bullseye, and the first person to raise their plush toy all the way to the top of the wall was the winner.

"When we were kids, my grandma used to give Mabel and me ten dollars each to play games at the fair. I remember thinking it was so much money back then."

"Tonight, I'm going to win you the big one," said Hugo.

He walked up to the Bushel Basket toss.

"Five dollars a ball or three balls for ten dollars," the carny called out.

Hugo handed him a ten-dollar bill and whipped all three balls toward the baskets in a matter of seconds. He missed every shot. Hugo dug more money from his jean pocket and handed the man a second ten-dollar bill. Sarah gently touched his shoulder. "Hugo, don't waste your money. I don't need a teddy. Most of these games are rigged anyway."

He shrugged her hand off his shoulder. "I got this."

He threw the first two balls, and both bounced out of the old bushel. He picked up the last ball and stood directly in front of the basket. He aimed for the top this time and tossed the ball with a sharp flick of his wrist. It dropped right into the basket.

"Yes!" he said, flexing. He kissed his biceps. "I told you I could do it."

Sarah laughed, but her laughter quickly gave way to shrieks when Hugo picked her up and twirled her around. "Put me down!" she cried, loving every minute of it.

The carny handed Hugo a teddy bear the size of a small child. "Congratulations, man."

Hugo put the cheap, plush prize on top of his shoulders and proudly walked through the fairgrounds with Sarah on his arm. They visited the agriculture exhibits, petted the goats, and fed the bunnies. Hugo was impressed by the town's prize pig. "That's over three-hundred pounds of bacon."

In the entertainment venue, they watched as a man on a motorcycle performed questionable stunts. His amateur performance made Sarah wonder if he had even practiced his act.

"It's getting dark. Let's go for a ride on the Ferris wheel," she said.

Sarah had wanted to save the best ride for last. While the spinning strawberries were the most fun, there was something magical and old-fashioned about the Ferris wheel. When she was little, her grandma would take them on the Ferris wheel when the sun began to set. Grandma would sit in the middle of the bench with Sarah on one side and Mabel on the other. Sarah loved to lean her flushed cheek into her grandma's cool, papery arm. After a long day of walking, rides, and endless glasses of lemonade, it was nice to curl up next to her grandma on the Ferris wheel.

"Step right up!" said the ride worker with a scorpion neck tattoo. Sarah and Hugo had reached the front of the line. "Two tickets please."

Hugo handed over a couple of blue tokens, and the man opened the bar to their bench. Hugo wrapped his arm around Sarah's shoulders, and she cuddled into the sweet spot against his chest. As their bench moved higher, the noise and excitement from the theme park below began to quiet. It was nice to have a moment to themselves.

"Wow," said Hugo. From the top of the ride, they had a spectacular view of the landscape around them. There was plenty of visual stimulation below with all the bright colored lights and people everywhere.

"There is nothing more romantic than riding on a Ferris wheel with someone you care about," said Sarah.

Hugo took her chin in his hand and tilted her face toward his. Her heart beat faster as Hugo's tanned face came down to meet hers. As the Ferris wheel lurched forward and picked up speed, Sarah reached her hand around his neck and pulled his soft, clean-shaven face to hers. The kiss was intense. Sarah had never realized how thrilling kissing could be until she was doing it on top of the world. It was as if fireworks were glowing inside of her. She felt explosively attracted to Hugo.

"Hey, you two, that will be another two tickets if you want to keep riding," the carny interrupted.

Hugo and Sarah finally came up for air and realized that not only had their ride reached the end of its journey, but they had become the evening entertainment for an audience of people waiting for their turn. Hugo grabbed Sarah's hand, and they made a dash for the exit.

"Did you see that woman's face?" said Hugo. He held his stomach, pretending that it hurt from laughing so hard.

"Oh, come on, we kept it PG." She winked at Hugo.

"All that kissing has made me hungry. Want to get something to eat?"

Sarah nodded and wrapped her arm around Hugo's waist. "Have you ever tried a corn dog?"

Sarah's mother thought fair food was the scariest part about a carnival. But to Sarah, it was all fun. Everything sold at the fair was deep-fried and covered in either salt or sugar. She instructed Hugo to go find them an empty picnic table and then she went around buying yummy snacks for her health-conscious hockey player to try. She returned to their table with a smorgasbord of treats. First, she passed Hugo a paper plate of steaming hot French fries that were drenched in brown gravy and sprinkled with cheese curds.

"What is this?"

"It's our famous Canadian dish, poutine. You have to try it."

"And that?" he said, pointing to a flat donut that was dipped in butter and sprinkled with cinnamon and sugar.

"A beavertail."

"What are you trying to do to me? I'm not going to be able to fit into these jeans tomorrow." He lifted his shirt and pointed to his concrete midsection.

"Oh, stop." Sarah rolled her eyes and reached for a gooey fry. "Mm," she said closing her eyes.

"Sarah!"

Her eyes snapped open, and she scanned the crowd. She'd know that voice anywhere.

"Hey, guys," yelled Scott. He marched up to their table as if he were on a mission. Britney trailed close behind like a loyal Labrador retriever.

"You didn't tell me you were coming tonight," said Sarah. She could tell he was high. His eyes were hooded and red.

Scott shrugged. "Last minute decision, I guess."

"I invited him," said Britney. She narrowed her eyes in Sarah's direction.

"Jeff, Shannon, and a couple of buddies from town are tailgating in the field by the demolition derby track," said Scott. "You guys should come. We have a cooler full of beer, and it's the best spot to watch the fireworks."

Sarah frowned.

"Yeah, buddy, that sounds great," said Hugo. "French fry?"

"Yeah, man, I'm starving." Scott sat down beside Sarah and reached for the poutine. He smelled skunky, like marijuana. Britney crossed her arms and stood awkwardly beside Scott.

"Here. You can have my seat," said Sarah to Britney. She got up and glared at Scott as she moved around the table to sit with Hugo. Scott was oblivious to her death stare and seemed only to care about the food in front of him.

"This is so good!" he said with his mouth full.

After Scott finished the rest of their carnival food, the four of them went to meet the group in the field. There they found Jeff, Shannon, and a few other people Sarah recognized from the bonfire party.

"Sarah!" Shannon shrieked. After a few beers, her voice was three octaves higher than normal. "I haven't seen you in, like, so long!"

Shannon wrapped an arm around Sarah's shoulders and batted her fake eyelashes at Hugo. "And who are you?" she said, eyeing Hugo like a hungry vixen ready to pounce on its prey.

"This is the guy I'm seeing," said Sarah. "Hugo, this is Shannon. We work together."

"Nice to meet you," said Hugo. His attentive

smile filled Sarah with jealousy.

"Sarah, come over here," Jeff called.

Sarah excused herself and sat down in the empty chair beside Jeff.

"Are you having a good time?" he asked.

"Well, I was until Scott ruined our romantic date." She crossed her arms and slumped down in the canvas seat.

"Aw, you're cute when you pout." He reached over and flicked her bottom lip so it bounced against her top lip, making a silly blubbery sound.

"Don't make fun of me," she whined. She swatted his hand away and sat up taller.

"Come on, Sarah. The night is young! There's still time to, you know…" He raised his eyebrows wildly to imply there was some naughty deeds afoot.

"I'm not so sure anymore." Sarah watched Hugo and Shannon. She was too far away to eavesdrop, but it was obvious Hugo was interested in whatever it was that Shannon had to say.

"Ignore her. Hugo is into you. He told me himself."

Sarah sighed. Jeff always had a way of calming her down. She reached over and gave his hand a grateful squeeze. "Enough about me. How are you doing? Have you heard from Julie?"

"Yeah, we talked on the phone for three hours last night."

Sarah wondered for a moment if she and Hugo had ever had a conversation that lasted longer than five minutes. They seemed to spend an awful lot of their time not talking.

"She's really great," said Jeff.

"But you hate talking on the phone."

"Not with Julie."

"You are head over heels!"

Jeff nodded sheepishly and pulled at the collar of his shirt.

"I'm happy for you guys. You deserve each other." Sarah noticed Jeff, the life of every party, didn't have a beer in hand. "You're not drinking tonight?"

"Naw, Scott decided to smoke with the townies, so I figured I'd be the responsible one. Somebody has to get his truck back to the cottage." Jeff looked at his watch. "Hey, guys!" he called out to his friends. "The fireworks are about to start."

Hugo made his way back to Sarah and stood behind her, massaging her neck. She looked up and smiled at him. Jeff was right. There was still plenty of time to get their date back on track. She stood up and gave Hugo a kiss on the cheek. "I'll be right back."

After excusing herself, Sarah hurried to find a porta-potty. She didn't want to miss the show. She spotted a lone toilet near the track bleachers. She pulled on the porta-potty's white handle, but noticed the red marker. Occupied. She hopped from foot to foot, waiting impatiently for whoever was inside to finish their business. Suddenly, Scott stumbled out from behind the bleachers with Britney in tow. His curly hair was a mess.

"Oh, hey, Sarah," he said. "We were just on a walk."

Sarah could tell from the purple hickey on his neck that Scott and Britney had been doing much more than walking.

"Come on, Scotty," said Britney in a breathy Marilyn Monroe voice. She nibbled on his ear lobe. "The fireworks are starting."

Scott shrugged her off. "I'll catch up with you in a minute."

Britney's shoulders slumped forward, and she

wandered toward the group like a lost puppy.

"Real nice, Scott."

"She'll be fine. Listen, I wanted to talk to you about Hugo."

"What about him?"

"I don't trust him. I mean, I like the guy, but I can tell he's a player."

Sarah crossed her arms and wished whoever was in the porta-potty would hurry the hell up. "Takes one to know one, I guess."

Scott drew his eyebrows together in a tormented expression. Sarah cradled her arms about her. She instantly regretted what she had said, but she was still too irritated with him to apologize. Scott gently placed his hand on her forearm. "I care about you, Sarah, more than you know. I just want you to be careful," he said in a resigned voice.

Suddenly, a firework exploded into a glittering silver shower above them. Sarah had tried to swallow her animosity, but as the next firework shot above them and shattered into a thousand sparks, so did her anger.

"What's it to you?" she yelled above the noise. "I don't need you to protect me, Scott. I'm not the same little girl who's afraid of the dark. I'm a grown woman! I can look out for myself."

"Sarah, I—"

Sarah held up her hand to cut him off. As far as she was concerned, their conversation was over. The person occupying the washroom stumbled out just in time. Tears had threatened to escape at any moment, and Sarah didn't want Scott to see her cry. Once she found solace in the washroom, heavy tears fell down her cheeks. She resented Scott for ruining her perfect date with Hugo. She hated that she'd felt pangs of jealousy when she saw the hickey on Scott's neck. Most of all, she was furious at herself for still loving Scott. Sarah's sobs were muffled by the next round of fireworks.

Chapter Eight

The next morning, Sarah borrowed her mom's car to get to work. She stared straight ahead as she passed the Roberts' cottage, but from the corner of her eye, she could see Scott was outside, waiting for her beside his truck.

Let him wait, she thought.

She gritted her teeth and pushed on the gas as her mind replayed the previous night's embarrassing debacle.

Once Sarah had pulled herself together in the washroom, she had awkwardly exited the phone-booth sized door and come face to face with Hugo. He had been waiting for her with his hands in his pockets.

"Are you okay?" he asked. His eyes were filled with concern. "Scott told me I should check up on you."

Sarah smiled as if her jaw was wired shut. "I'm fine."

He took her hand. "Okay, let's head back to the group then."

Sarah pulled her hand away. She couldn't stop thinking about Scott's warning. She also didn't have it in her to watch Britney and Scott make out all night. "Actually, Hugo," she said placing her hand on her forehead. "I'm not feeling that well. Do you mind taking me home?"

"Of course." Hugo wrapped his arm around her and led her back to the Roberts' station wagon. She appreciated his kindness. It proved Scott wrong. Her tired legs felt weak, and she leaned into him for support.

Now, on the way to work, her sadness had been replaced with anger. She gripped the steering wheel and took the bends in the road as if she were a drag racer. She was furious with Scott for putting doubts in her mind about Hugo and ruining her date. She was also angry with herself for still having lingering feelings for Scott.

She screeched into the beach parking lot and pulled into an empty spot. She turned off the ignition, got out of the car, grabbed her duffle bag from the trunk, and marched to the staff changeroom. It was empty. She stepped into her one-piece bathing suit and then pulled on her matching green shorts over the top. She collected her long hair into a ponytail and slipped her red whistle around her neck.

On her way to the adjoining ladies' room, she heard Shannon and Britney's voices and quickly stepped into a stall.

"I don't know what his problem is," said Britney. "We were having a good time. He was totally into it until he saw her walk by. I think Scott secretly has a thing for her."

"Tell me about it," said Shannon. "Hugo and I were, like, in the middle of a great conversation when Scott suddenly appears, whispers in his ear, and poor Hugo has to go tend to the party pooper."

"I could totally tell Hugo was into you," said Britney. "There was definitely some chemistry there."

"I felt it, too!" said Shannon. "At one point, he even had his arm around my shoulders."

"He's so hot."

"His body is like rock hard."

"Well, it looks like you'll be the only one getting some this summer. Get on it, girl."

Shannon and Britney laughed as they left the changeroom. Sarah sat in her stall in disbelief. Every word out of Shannon's mouth fueled the fire that burned inside of her. Sarah slammed open the stall door, left the changeroom in a huff, and marched straight to the lifeguard shack.

"Kurt, I need to talk to you."

He put down his clipboard, giving her his full attention. "What can I do for you, chickee?"

"I'm not feeling very well. I need to take a sick day."

"You just started working here yesterday."

Sarah bit her lip. She didn't want to risk losing her job. She needed the money, but she also needed a clear head to lifeguard properly. "I know. I'm sorry for the inconvenience—"

"You don't look sick."

Sarah crossed her arms. "Cramps," she lied.

Kurt's sunburned skin turned a deeper shade of lobster red. He nodded, then picked up his clipboard and began restocking the first aid kits with Band-Aids.

Sarah thoroughly enjoyed watching him squirm. "I'll see you tomorrow, Kurt."

The familiar scent of the pine floor in the cottage was comforting. Sarah kicked off her sandy flip-flops and dropped her duffle bag on a kitchen chair before opening the refrigerator. She poured herself a tall glass of iced tea and joined her mother outside on the deck.

"Oh, you're home. I wasn't expecting you until dinner," said Mom from her lounge chair. She placed her book in her lap. "Everything okay?"

Sarah nodded. "They switched the schedule and forgot to tell me."

"Wonderful! I mean, now we can spend the whole day together. Mabel isn't working until the dinner shift."

"Actually Mom, I was going to use this time to write. I was thinking a solo paddle might clear my head first."

Her mom smiled halfheartedly. "Okay, honey."

Sarah winced. She hated disappointing her mother. "What if we went out for dinner tonight? We could make Mabel wait on us at Fiddleheads and then surprise her by leaving a big ol' tip."

"Well, that sounds like fun. I'll be ready by 5:00."

Sarah packed a peanut butter and banana sandwich, an apple, and a water bottle into her backpack. She slipped her notebook and extra pencils into a Ziplock bag to protect them from getting wet. As she swung her bag onto her back, the beige phone on the kitchen wall rang. She picked up its heavy receiver. "Hello?"

"Sarah?"

"Oh, hi, Daddy."

"Hey, sweet pea. Listen, my flight arrives in Ottawa tomorrow afternoon at 2:00. Tell your mother I'm going to rent a car. There is no need to pick me up. If there aren't any delays, I should be at the cottage in time for dinner."

"Why don't you tell her yourself? I'll go get her. I know she would be happy to talk—"

"Actually, I'm about to step into another meeting. I'll see you tomorrow, hun." Click.

Sarah hung up the receiver. Her father was in such a rush these days. Always busy. She hated that he couldn't spare five minutes to talk to Mom.

On her way down to the dock, Sarah told her mother the news.

"He didn't want to talk to me?" Mom pressed her lips into a thin line, and her forehead wrinkled with concern.

"He was late for a meeting, Mom. He said he'd be here for dinner tomorrow."

"I'll make his favorite."

Sarah kissed her mom on the crown of her head and continued down the steep stairs to the dock.

Her dad had taught her that when paddling a canoe solo, she should sit up front, facing the stern. This would help prevent the boat from zigzagging all over the lake. She tossed her gear into the green canoe, knelt on the bottom of the boat, and employed her rock-solid stroke.

Sarah loved the sense of freedom that paddling solo gave her. She could maneuver the boat as fast as she wanted without the hassle of coordinating strokes with a partner. The best part of paddling alone was that she could go wherever she wanted. Every stroke took her deeper into her journey. Being on the water, completely immersed in nature, her senses became acute. She loved watching the warm yellow light of the sun bounce off the glassy lake, and she could taste the humidity on her tongue as she panted through each stroke. The muscles in her arms protested, but Sarah kept planting the paddle blade in the water and propelling the canoe forward.

When she reached the tip of the river, Sarah placed her paddle in the boat and sat on the floor of the canoe with her legs stretched out in front of her. Her knees were red and dry from kneeling. She removed her notebook and a yellow pencil from the Ziplock bag and began writing. Fresh air seemed to be the key to unlocking her ideas from her brain vault. As her canoe slowly drifted down the narrow waterway, her jumbled thoughts turned into coherent sentences. Playing hooky to have a carefree day on the lake was just what she'd needed. Sarah chewed on the tiny eraser on the end of her pencil. It squeaked between her teeth. As she floated past the reeds, memories of her childhood summers flooded her mind.

Jeff had always called the river "the bayou" because it was slow-moving and had a swampy section that was perfect for spotting turtles.

"I see one!" Jeff had said one summer afternoon when Sarah was ten. He'd pointed to a turtle basking on a black rock near the water's edge. "Right there! It's a painted turtle."

"How can you tell?" Sarah had asked, struggling to steer the canoe straight.

"Because it has red, yellow, and orange stripes on it."

They'd tried to paddle in unison to move the heavy canoe through the thick lily pads towards the turtle.

Jeff had grabbed his fishing net. "Hold steady," he'd whispered.

He had stood up in the boat, ready to catch it, but Sarah didn't have the strength to paddle the boat on her own, and the canoe steered the wrong way. Determined to catch the turtle, Jeff had reached out, but lost his balance. He'd splashed into the swamp, almost taking Sarah with him. She'd held onto the sides of the canoe as it violently rocked back and forth.

"Get me out of here," Jeff had cried.

He'd swam toward the canoe with pieces of slime and sludge stuck in his white-blond hair. In order to get her best friend back in the boat, Sarah had to lean to one side to help balance the canoe. Jeff flung his leg over the opposite side and rolled back in. He'd escaped the whole ordeal with two leeches stuck to his right ankle. The incident later transformed into quite the tall tale for Jeff to tell at campfires for years to come.

Now, alone in the same canoe, Sarah shivered as she remembered how close she had come that day to being lunch for the ugly blood suckers that crawled in the swampy water below. Sarah wasn't wearing a watch, but she could tell from the position of the sun that she must have been writing for a while. Pleased with her efforts, she placed her notebook and pencil back in the Ziplock bag and picked up her paddle, ready to return to the cottage.

On the way back, small waves hit the sides of the

canoe, wafting the earthy smell of the lake water into Sarah's uplifted face. When the unwanted thoughts of Scott and Hugo began to play all over again, Sarah refused to allow herself to dwell on them. She had decided she would just ask Hugo point-blank if he was interested in Shannon the next time she saw him.

Sarah was navigating the boat across the bay back to the cottage when she saw Hugo fishing off the Roberts' dock. He grinned ear to ear when he saw her. "Hey, beautiful!"

Sarah waved back tentatively. "Catch anything?"

"Not yet. Come and join me."

Sarah maneuvered the canoe parallel to the side of the Roberts' dock. Hugo stabilized the boat for her as she climbed out.

"Are you feeling better today?" Hugo asked. He took the yellow rope that was tied to the bow of the canoe and secured the unmanned boat to the dock. Sarah wiped her hands on her shorts. "I took the day off. I'm feeling much better now, thanks."

Hugo smiled and passed her a fishing rod and a Styrofoam container full of earthworms. He raised his fishing rod above his head and made a cast while Sarah dug through the dirt for some juicy bait. She speared a slippery worm and slid it up the hook. With the container of worms at her feet, Sarah pulled the rod tip back over her right shoulder. She released the line with her finger and cast the rod forward. Sarah really didn't care if she caught anything that day—she was fishing for something else.

"Shannon seems nice."

Hugo nodded as he reeled in a long piece of seaweed.

"She's very pretty," Sarah added.

Hugo looked up at Sarah before he removed the

tangled mess of green off his hook and threw it back into the lake.

"Are you okay?" he asked.

Sarah cringed. She knew she sounded desperate. She wasn't particularly good at confrontation. She reeled in her line and placed her rod down on the dock.

"I overheard Shannon talking about last night in the locker room at the lifeguard station. She's definitely into you. Are you interested in her?"

Hugo cocked his head and wrinkled his nose. "Nothing happened last night. We were just talking."

Sarah let out a sigh of relief. A slow smile spread across her face. Hugo put down his fishing rod and placed his hands on Sarah's shoulders. He lowered his eyebrows as if he were trying to organize his thoughts. He frowned. "We're having a fun summer together, right?"

"Yes, definitely." Sarah stood on her tip toes, eager to kiss his generous lips, but he held her back. She landed on her heels with a thump.

"Sarah, I think you are wonderful, but I need to be honest with you."

The relief that had washed over her moments ago now trickled down her spine.

"I don't want to disrespect you or the Roberts family because I know you are important to them." Hugo took a deep breath. "I guess, I'm just a little worried about where you think this is going and how you're feeling."

Sarah swallowed the lump in her throat. "I hadn't thought too far ahead, but I guess in the back of my mind I've always known we'd be going our separate ways at the end of the summer."

Hugo nodded.

"Different schools, different provinces," she

continued.

"Exactly," he said. "So, we're on the same page?"

Sarah nodded. Even though she had thought it was possible to find long-term love in July, it was clear that it wasn't in Hugo's plans.

"I want to have fun," he said. "Are you still open to that?"

His words stung. Sarah knew she cared about Hugo and worried that her feelings for him would grow between now and Labor Day. She looked into Hugo's honest eyes and decided to ignore the red flags that warned her that being friends with benefits was a terrible idea. Sarah wanted to have a fun summer, and Hugo was the full package of adventure and easygoing-ness that she didn't think had existed before now.

"Yes, Hugo. I'm still open to that."

"I'm so relieved." He wrapped his arms around her in a tight bear hug. "Do you want to go into town for some ice cream?"

Sarah untied the yellow rope from the dock and tossed it into her canoe. "I can't. I have a dinner date with my mom tonight. Next time?"

"Definitely."

Hugo held the side of the canoe against the dock as Sarah stepped back in and kneeled at the bow. Hugo kissed her on the cheek and pushed her in the direction of her cottage. "See you later, beautiful."

Paddling all day without a partner had been a challenge, but as Sarah made her way back to her dock all on her own, she came to the realization that maybe she didn't need a serious relationship after all.

I can paddle my own damn canoe.

ALYSSA DELLE PALME

Chapter Nine

The next day, Sarah watched as her mom fretted around the cottage in her yoga pants, getting everything ready for her dad's arrival.

"I don't know why you're making such a fuss. It's just dad," said Sarah.

"He's been away for months. He works so hard he deserves to have a nice vacation."

"Of course. I just don't think you need to stress about cleaning every nook and cranny. The cottage is clean."

"I want everything to be perfect." Her mother handed her a mop. "You can wash the floors. I have to change the bedding."

Sweat dripped down Sarah's sports bra as she helped her mother with the chores. The sun was beating down on the roof of the cottage, and the thermometer had already reached 30 degrees Celsius, heating the place up like an oven. She longed to go for a dip in the lake to cool down, but she knew her mother had a long list of preparations. Mabel got off easy. She was working the lunch shift at the restaurant.

"I went to the butcher," her mother had said over dinner at Fiddleheads Pub the night before. "I bought steaks for your dad. Do you think I should marinate them?"

Sarah shrugged. "I don't think it matters. Dad loves your cooking."

Mabel approached their table with a receipt in hand. She wore an all-black uniform—black jeans, black Keds, and a black Fiddleheads t-shirt. Her blonde hair was neatly tied back and styled with a silk polka-dot scarf. Mabel placed the receipt on the table with a handful of mints.

"There's no rush," she said politely, but from the look of the lineup out the door, it was time to wrap up dinner.

Mom took her wallet out and placed sixty dollars on the table for a thirty-dollar tab. "I won't be needing any change."

Mabel's eyes lit up.

"Really? Thanks for coming!" She smiled at Sarah and gave her mom a quick kiss on the cheek before hurrying away to check on a neighboring table.

Sarah's stomach grumbled as she thought about the previous night's chicken Caesar salad. She stopped scrubbing the kitchen floor and checked the clock on the stove. Noon.

"Mom!" Sarah called out. "Can we make lunch?"

Her mother came into the kitchen and washed her hands. "There's no time. I have to prep supper. She put on her apron. "If you're hungry, there's leftover pasta salad in the fridge."

Sarah opened the refrigerator, now stocked with her dad's favorite foods. She grabbed the summer salad and sat at the kitchen table to eat. Meanwhile, her mother marinated the steaks, washed the potatoes, peeled the corn, made a green salad, and put a bottle of white wine in the fridge to chill. For dessert, she had picked up a chocolate mousse cake from a local baker in town.

"I read once that chocolate has aphrodisiacal qualities," she told Sarah.

Sarah covered her ears. "Mom!"

"What? I miss being intimate with your father. He's been away, working around the clock, for three months. When he did have time to call home, it was a quick conversation, mostly pleasantries and discussions about bills or house chore to-do lists. I'm craving a warmer conversation and quality time with him. To be honest, I'm itching to communicate in other ways, too."

"Enough!" said Sarah. She didn't want to hear another word.

"Some of the best conversations are not always spoken," her mother continued.

Sarah stood up and placed her dirty bowl in the sink. She grabbed the linen tablecloth that her mother had ironed and went outside to set the picnic table. Sarah added four place settings and a vase of cheerful flowers that her mother had picked up at the farmer's market. Mom joined her outside and decorated the center of the table with beeswax tea lights. Sarah stood back to admire their work. The surrounding natural greenery made the space look like a beautiful summer retreat.

"It's perfect!" Mom said. "I have some primping to do. Will you help me choose an outfit?"

Sarah thought of a few things she'd rather do with her time, but she hadn't seen her mother this happy in months. She reluctantly agreed. While her mother showered and blow-dried her short blonde hair, Sarah went into her mother's closet and selected a dreamy white maxi dress made out of soft ramie. The dress was light, airy, and a little sexy with its deep V-neck and drawstring tie. Mom put on her turquoise teardrop earrings and dabbed her father's favorite perfume along her collarbone. The smell of ripe figs, creamy coconut milk, and caramelized brown sugar filled the bedroom.

"This perfume makes your dad crazy," Mom said.

Sarah rolled her eyes.

"Honey, you should be happy that your parents enjoy each other's company. I hope that one day, you, too, will have this sort of emotional and physical relationship with a partner."

For a brief moment, Sarah allowed herself to

imagine what it would be like to have that sort of relationship. In her daydream, it wasn't Hugo she envisioned spending her life with. It was Scott. She imagined they'd have a cottage wedding. Scott would look devastatingly handsome in a black tuxedo with his bowtie slightly crooked. Sarah would wear her mother's flowy bohemian style wedding dress and a daisy flower crown. She would walk down the aisle barefoot and they'd say their vows at the end of the Roberts' dock in front of all their friends and family.

"What are you two talking about?" Mabel asked, interrupting Sarah's thoughts. Mabel leaned against the door frame. Her work uniform was stained with small spots of grease.

"Great! You're back," Mom said, ignoring Mabel's question. She gave Mabel a quick peck on the cheek. "Go get changed. Your dad will be here soon."

An hour later, Sarah and Mabel were sitting outside on the deck, enjoying some appetizers as they waited for their father to arrive. Mom fretted around the picnic table, straightening the cutlery, and lighting the candles. When he finally walked through the sliding glass door, their jaws dropped.

"Daddy!" Mabel rushed over to him and threw her arms around his neck. "You look amazing."

"Wow, Dad! You look great," Sarah said, joining the group embrace.

"Jack, you must have lost twenty pounds," said Mom. She leaned in for a kiss, but Dad quickly lifted his chin and planted a peck on her forehead.

"Your dear old dad has been working out." He patted his midsection where his beer belly used to be.

"You look fantastic, Jack." Mom grabbed the bottle of chilled white wine from the picnic table, poured a generous glass and handed it to him. "Dinner is just about ready. Why don't you all sit down?"

Sarah, Mabel, and their father took their seats at the dinner table as Mom opened the lid of the barbeque. The steaks sizzled on the grill. They were golden brown and slightly charred, cooked to perfection.

"No steak for me," said Dad. "I'm a vegetarian now."

All three women stared at him in disbelief. Before he left for B.C., Dad was practically a carnivore. Mom left his steak on the grill and filled his plate with vegetables.

"I wish you had told me," said Mom as she served him his dinner. "I would have marinated you a portobello mushroom."

"No need to fuss over me. Can you please pass the salad?"

Mom handed Dad the bowl. Sarah knew not to pass him the salad dressing.

"I like to taste the vegetables," Dad had told her once when she was a child.

Dad squeezed a bit of fresh lemon juice overtop his salad. At 47, he still had a head full of brown hair. Sarah leaned her head against her dad's shoulder. She liked that she took after her father with his dark brown eyes and olive skin tone.

"You may look more like your father, but I like to think you inherited your passion and creativity from me," Mom would often remind her.

"How's your writing going?" Dad asked Sarah.

"I've been writing every day like you suggested."

"What are you working on? I would love to read something while I'm here."

"A series of short stories, but it's not ready yet."

"I'm looking forward to getting my hands on it." Dad bumped shoulders with Sarah, making her smile. He had always encouraged her creativity.

"Thanks, Dad. Your support means a lot to me."

"Just dedicate your first novel to me." Dad winked.

A bottle of wine later, Dad reached across the table and put his hand on top of Mabel's. "I'm sorry I wasn't there when everything fell apart with Benny."

Sarah glanced at her mother, who looked like she wanted to kick him under the table for bringing up a sensitive topic. "Um, Jack could you please pass the—"

"I'm fine, Daddy. Really."

Dad ignored Mom's glare. "Mabel, it's not healthy to keep your feelings bottled up inside. I'm here now if you ever need to talk about it. I'm a good listener."

Mabel nodded and shoved a piece of steak in her mouth.

"I could also take you out to do something fun, just us, to take your mind off things."

Mabel swallowed. "Actually, I've been wanting to go to the Movies Under the Stars. They're playing that new one with Julia Roberts."

"Consider it a date," said Dad. "We'll get all the fixings too—popcorn, slush puppies, and milk duds."

"I thought you were on a diet?" Mom asked. She collected their cutlery and polished-off plates.

"I can still enjoy a treat now and then with my girls. I'm on vacation."

Sarah helped her mom carry the pile of dishes inside and dumped them in the kitchen sink.

"Great!" Mom muttered under her breath. She swung the refrigerator door open. "Because I picked up your favorite dessert from the Little Creek Bakery."

Sarah and her mom returned moments later with four dessert plates piled high with chocolate mousse cake. Mom had added wild raspberries on top that she had picked herself from the bushes on their land.

"None for me, thanks," said Dad, patting his stomach. "I'm full."

Mom sat back down at the table with a huff. She grabbed her dessert spoon and shoveled a creamy glob of mousse into her mouth. Sarah struggled with the awkwardness of the moment. She barely recognized her dad, and when it came to her mom, he was acting aloof. Something was off.

ALYSSA DELLE PALME

Chapter Ten

After dinner, Sarah flopped onto her bed and closed her eyes, falling deep into a food coma. She was awakened minutes later when she heard loud voices coming through the thin walls. She slipped out of bed, tiptoed to the door, and opened it a crack. She could see her mother standing at the kitchen sink with her hands on her hips.

"Everything is fine," said Dad. He grabbed a dripping plate from the rack and dried it with a dish towel.

"You've barely made eye contact with me since you arrived," said Mom. She wiped a piece of wispy hair out of her face with the back of her rubber glove. "Is there something you're not telling me?"

"Why are you trying to start a fight?"

"Why are you answering my question with a question?"

"You're out of your mind. For fucks sake, Alice! I've been here for an hour, and you're already giving me grief."

Sarah winced at his harshness. Her mother's skin turned red from her neck to the roots of her blonde hair before she bit her lip and went back to scrubbing the dishes.

"I don't know what you want from me," Dad said, rubbing his eyes.

Mom looked down at the sink. "Is there a reason you're not paying attention to me?"

"You're officially losing it. How the hell am I supposed to pay attention to you when I'm working on the other side of the damn country?"

"For starters, a phone call that lasted longer than

five minutes every now and again would've been nice."

"I was working! How do you think our bills get paid? Who is paying to put the girls through university? And this is the thanks I get?" Dad shook his head and raised his hands in frustration. "It's not like you're contributing to our financial picture."

"I have dedicated my whole life to this family. The only reason you have a successful career in the first place is because I stayed home. I looked after our children. I made all your meals. I kept the house clean!" Mom ripped the rubber gloves off her hands and threw them on the counter. She marched out of the kitchen with Dad on her tail.

Moments later, Sarah heard the slam of a bedroom door and then the start of an ignition outside. She bounced over her bed to the window and peeked through the sheer white curtains. Her father took off down the driveway in his rented red sports car. She wondered if he would come back. Hearing her parents argue made her nauseated. She was thinking about checking on her mother when her bedroom door creaked open. Mabel poked her head in. "Do you want to get out of here?" she whispered.

Sarah nodded. She grabbed a sweatshirt from behind her door and followed Mabel out of the cottage and down the steps to the end of their dock. They sat silently side by side with their feet dangling above the water. A ladybug landed on Sarah's knee. Its bright red back caught her attention, nature's warning sign. Before this moment, she had never realized that a ladybug's black spots were symmetrical. Sarah scooped up the tiny insect and brought her over to the leaning birch tree that grew out of moss-covered rocks. She placed the ladybug in the surrounding bed of green ferns.

"Do you think Mom and Dad will be okay?"

Mabel asked.

Sarah rejoined her sister at the end of the dock. The lake was calm, but ripples appeared in different directions every time the breeze blew.

"I think Dad might be going through a midlife crisis," said Sarah.

"Why do you say that?"

"His new look, red sports car. It's obvious."

"What? No way. The car is a rental, and he's finally taking good care of himself. Mom should be happy he looks so good."

Sarah shrugged. "Mom is grieving, and Dad hasn't made himself available to her."

"He has a job, Sarah."

"I understand that, but Mom needed extra support this year."

"All she does it mope around. Dad just got here, and she's already breathing down his neck. I would be mad, too. He's been working long hours to complete his contract with the government. He needs a break."

"I think she's lonely is all."

Mabel rested her head against Sarah's shoulder. "I know how that feels."

"You're getting stronger every minute, Mabel." Sarah wrapped her arm around her sister's shoulders.

"It still hurts," Mabel said, wiping a tear off her cheek with her finger.

"You won't always feel this way."

Mabel sat up straight and pulled her knees into her chest. "I read in one of Mom's *Cosmopolitan* magazines that the best way to get over someone is to get under someone else."

"Mabel!"

"Oh, don't be such a prude. I think a rebound might be just what I need to get over Benny."

"Do you have someone in mind?"

"Scott."

"As in our friend Scott? Scott Roberts?"

"Yes, and before you get your panties in a bunch, hear me out. First of all, he's hot. Second of all, Scott is a player. He's not looking for anything serious, and neither am I."

"But you guys are friends. Good friends. Once you cross that line—"

"I know it sounds risky, but it might be fun. A no-strings-attached situation."

Sarah squirmed in her seat. In the rules of girl code, dating your sister's crush was a huge no-no, but she couldn't fault Mabel for that because she was totally unaware of Sarah's feelings for Scott.

"I actually think this might be my best idea yet," said Mabel.

"Lots of disasters seem like the best idea."

"I thought you'd be more supportive."

Sarah looked into her sister's sad brown eyes. "Things will be forever changed, Mabel. If it doesn't work out, you'll never get your friend back."

"Girls!" called their dad. Sarah and Mabel looked up to see their father leaning against the railing on the top landing of the stairs. He held up a plastic MJ's Convenience Store bag full of junk food. "Mabel, I bought all your favorite treats." He checked his watch. "It's 8:30. The movie starts in half an hour. Let's go!"

Sarah was relieved their father had come back. She wondered if he had made up with Mom. MJ's Convenience Store was a short drive away and only sold three things—candy, ice cream and worms for fishing. MJ's was also accessible by boat, but it took a lot longer to get there in their canoe. When Sarah and Mabel were younger, they often paddled to the store with their allowance burning a hole in their pockets. They'd buy two scoops of rocky road and eat their treat on MJ's dock.

"Do you want to come to the movie with us?" Mabel asked Sarah.

"No, this is your date with Dad. Thanks for the invite."

"Suit yourself." Mabel stood and dusted herself off. In a desperate attempt to get through to her sister, Sarah grabbed hold of Mabel's hand. "If you get together with Scott, you're heading down a road with no U-turn. Don't hook up with him."

"You worry too much." Mabel bent down and gave Sarah a quick peck on the cheek. "You're sweet for looking out for me."

Sarah stayed at the end of the dock and watched the sun set behind the pine trees across the bay. The sky was a swirl of electric pink and orange. Birdsong swelled around her as the nocturnal musicians sung from their high perches above, while the frogs and crickets added an eerie overture in the marsh at the end of the bay.

A burst of loneliness washed over Sarah like the big waves that suddenly submerged her feet that dangled off the dock. Distracted by her own thoughts, Sarah hadn't noticed the motorboat as it passed by, making waves. She lifted her dripping feet. The cool breeze numbed her wet toes. She pulled her oversize sweatshirt over her knees and tucked in her cold feet.

The thought of Mabel and Scott together made Sarah cringe. On one hand, a rebound could be the oar that might help Mabel paddle back into the dating world. On the other hand, Sarah didn't know how she was going to squash her sister's plans to seduce her crush. Sarah couldn't be honest about her feelings for Scott either, for all the same reasons she had told Mabel it was a bad idea.

ALYSSA DELLE PALME

Unless he really is the one.

Chapter Eleven

"Sarah, wake up," her father whispered in her ear.

Sarah rubbed her eyes and looked around her dark room. "What time is it?"

"6:00," he said, checking his watch. "I thought we could go for a sunrise paddle together."

Sarah uncurled her body and stretched it as long as she could make it, pointing her toes and yawning. She let out a big breath and nodded. "Okay."

"Get ready, and I'll bring the paddle boards down to the dock. I'll meet you back up here to help you with the lifejackets and paddles."

Sarah stumbled around her dark room, looking for something to wear. She pulled on a pair of black, lightweight running shorts and a neon pink, high-neck sports bra. She tiptoed to the bathroom and tossed her tangled hair up in a messy bun. She was midway through brushing her teeth when she heard murmurs coming from the kitchen. She opened the bathroom door a crack. Her father was talking to someone on the phone. Sarah spit into the sink and wiped the remaining toothpaste foam off her lips with the hand towel that hung on the rack. She quietly opened the bathroom door and crept into the hallway.

"No, I haven't told them yet," Dad whispered.

The old pine floors gave Sarah away as they creaked beneath her feet. Her father hung up the phone in haste and peeked around the corner.

"All set, hun?"

Sarah smiled weakly and nodded.

It must have been a work crisis, she thought in her sleepy haze. It made sense with the time difference. Despite being on vacation, her dad still had to carry a pager for work.

Sarah's favorite time to go paddle boarding was early in the morning when the lake was still and the fog hadn't yet burned off. Sarah stood tall as she paddled. It felt as if she were walking on water, but better because she was gliding. Paddle boarding was a relatively new sport in the area. Her dad had brought back the pair of boards from a work trip in Hawaii a couple of years earlier. They were the only family on the lake to own a set of paddle boards.

Sarah began her workout with slow gentle strokes. With the water under her feet, she had an amazing viewpoint to watch the fish swimming below. Once the muscles of her body were awake, she pushed herself to get her heart rate up. The goal was to beat her dad to the imaginary finish line, which was always out of the bay and into the middle of the lake. She focused on keeping her body balanced and her mind eased into meditation. Her mind and body were one with the board.

"You've been practicing," said Sarah breathlessly. She met her dad across the finish line, where he was patiently waiting for her, sitting cross-legged on his board. Sarah sat down on her board and closed her eyes, listening to the sounds of nature as her tired lungs filled with fresh country air.

"It's been my escape from the daily grind in B.C," he said. "Though paddle boarding in the ocean is more difficult. You'll have to try it when you come out west to visit your dear ol' dad someday."

"I thought your contract was only for six months?"

"Uh… I only meant if my contract gets extended or if my position becomes permanent."

"Permanent? Ha! Good luck getting Mom to move to B.C. She hates the rain."

Dad nodded and fixed his gaze on the horizon.

His mood turned quiet.

"I love it out there. It's my home. Did you know I've been begging your mother to move there since we got married?"

Sarah was worrying she had said something wrong when, suddenly, she heard soft grunts nearby. Sarah looked toward the shoreline and saw something dark and sleek swimming along. The animal raised its neck far out of the water.

"Dad, look! An otter."

They watched as the otter with its short, rich chocolate brown fur playfully rolled and dove back into the lake.

"Do you remember when I used to call you my otter pup?" her dad asked.

Sarah smiled. She had earned the nickname when she was younger because she was the family's star swimmer.

"Even on the coldest of summer mornings, I'd ask, 'Who wants to go for a swim across the bay?' and you would always shout an enthusiastic 'Me!'" said Dad.

"I did it for the post-swim hot chocolate reward," said Sarah.

"What?" he said, pretending to be offended. "I always thought it was for the chance to spend time with me."

Sarah laughed. "Do you remember the summer I spent two weeks lugging around heavy stones to help you build a retaining wall for the septic tank? I definitely did that just to spend time with you."

Dad smiled. "What do you say, pup? Should we go for a dip?"

Sarah grinned. They both slowly stood up on the ends of their paddle boards and dove into the lake like a pair of synchronized swimmers. The water was frigid, but

Sarah didn't mind. She was simply happy to be out in nature, reconnecting with her dad.

"I think I owe you a hot chocolate," Dad said after he popped up for air.

It wasn't until they had paddled back to the cottage that Sarah, now wide awake and thinking clearly, remembered that the 3-hour time difference between British Columbia and Ontario put B.C. behind Ontario, not ahead. In her early morning haze, she had gotten this confused. Sarah's heart sank as she realized that her father's phone call couldn't have been work related because she knew full well that government offices in B.C. were not open for business at 3:00 in the morning.

Who had he been talking to?

Sarah felt queasy as she helped her dad carry the paddle boards back to their rack. Her hands trembled as she picked up her lifejacket and paddle. She thought about an episode she had watched on *Oprah* once where a marriage counsellor revealed how common infidelity was among married couples.

"Dad, did you know that one in two-point-seven men cheat, and most wives never find out about it?"

When her dad didn't respond, Sarah wasn't sure if he had heard her or not. Her nausea mounted with every step back up to the cottage deck. When she reached the top, she sat down at the picnic table and put her head between her knees. Her heart pounded in her ears.

"Do you know why Molly isn't at school today?" Julie had whispered to Sarah earlier that year in their busy Catholic high school hallway. Sarah shook her head. Molly usually sat at their lunch table in the cafeteria, but her seat was empty that day. Julie was friends with her through the school's drama club. Molly was more of an acquaintance to Sarah.

"I called her on my spare period because we're

partners for a presentation in our musical theater class today," Julie said. She looked around to make sure no one was eavesdropping. Sarah leaned in closer. "Her parents are getting a divorce."

"That's so sad," said Sarah. "Weren't they volunteers for the marriage preparation course through their church?"

Sarah remembered Molly distinctly complaining about how her parents invited strangers into their home every Thursday night to lead a course that was designed to help couples prepare for the sacrament of marriage. Molly's parents volunteered her to make the tea and serve digestive cookies midway through the program. Molly hated it.

"Yeah. Her dad left her mom for their neighbor," said Julie. "She's a divorcee with fake tits."

When Molly eventually came back to school, she returned as a goth. She had dyed her pretty blonde hair black and wore black lipstick and Dr. Martens boots. Sarah supposed it was Molly's way of getting back at her father. Or perhaps, she was dressing like how she felt on the inside. Either way, Sarah knew she never wanted to be the victim of divorced parents.

"Sarah, are you OK?" Mom asked.

Her dad reached the top of the stairs moments later. "What's the matter?"

Sarah looked up. Her eyesight was blurry. She put her head back between her knees. "I think I worked out too hard, and I haven't had anything to eat this morning."

"Low blood sugar," said Mom. She ran inside and brought back a tall glass of orange juice. "Sip this slowly. It will make you feel better."

Dad placed his hand on Sarah's shoulder. "You okay, kiddo?"

"Mmhmm." She refused to look at him.

"Good. I'm going to go shower. Great paddle this morning." Her dad patted her on the back and waltzed into the cottage without a worry in the world.

Sarah gritted her teeth and pulled her mom down to sit beside her. "Dad is up to something," Sarah whispered. "He was on the phone with someone early this morning."

As soon as she blurted it out, Sarah agonized over her decision. Maybe she had made the whole thing up, and this was just a big misunderstanding. Sarah felt close to tears. "It was probably work, right?" Sarah asked, begging her mother to reassure her.

Mom stood and marched inside the cottage. Sarah followed and watched as her mother looked around like a detective with a search warrant. Her mom went into her bedroom and came back moments later with Dad's briefcase. She slammed the sleek, brown leather briefcase down on the kitchen table and worked to unlock it. It popped open on the first try.

Sarah stared at its soft suede lining as her mother flipped through piles of papers. Suddenly, a lone photograph fell from the stack of papers and fluttered down to the ground like the last leaf on a tree in autumn. Alice bent and looked at the photo closely. She bit her lip and then covered her face with her hands.

"What is it?" Sarah asked.

Her mother didn't say a word but held out the photograph for Sarah to see for herself. It was a recent picture of her dad, standing trim and tanned in front of a sailboat in B.C. In the photo, he was smiling with his arm wrapped around a woman's waist. She was looking up at Dad in the photo, and her hand rested on his bare chest. She was younger, but not nearly as pretty as her mom. She was the polar opposite with tanned skin and short black hair.

She looks like a horse, Sarah thought.

"It says something on the back," Mom said.

Sarah flipped the photograph over. "Je t'aime. Emilee," Sarah read aloud.

"She's French?" Mom asked.

"She's in love with him," Sarah answered. She had studied enough French throughout high school to understand that Emilee had written *I love you.* They both stopped when they heard the shower turn off. Mom stood up and quickly stuffed everything back into the briefcase.

"What's all the commotion about?" Mabel said. She emerged from her bedroom, rubbing the sleep out of her eyes.

"Dad's having an affair," Sarah said. She handed the evidence to her sister. "Mom, what are you going to do?"

"I'm going to confront him, that's what."

Sarah stood bewildered in the middle of the kitchen. It felt as if her whole world was collapsing around her, and she was the one who had pressed the detonator. Sarah and Mabel retreated to the living room and sat still on the sofa. There, they watched their parents' marriage fall apart before their eyes.

"Are you having an affair?" Mom asked Dad as he excited the bathroom with a towel tied around his waist. Water dripped from the ends of his dark hair onto his shoulders.

"You're imagining things," Dad said. He went into the master bedroom and emerged moments later wearing a pair of gray jogging pants. He had a blue t-shirt in hand. "You sound crazy. You know that, don't you?"

"Who's Emilee?"

Dad stopped in his tracks.

"She's a friend from work," he said after a long pause. "You're so paranoid. You know that's just because you're so insecure." Dad stuck his toned arms through the t-shirt and aggressively pulled it over his head.

"Did I also imagine the fact that you've moved to B.C?" Mom crossed her arms. "Permanently?"

The color drained from Dad's tanned face. "Not in front of the girls," he whispered.

Mom flung an arm in Sarah and Mabel's direction. "They're adults! They deserve to know what's going on." Mom clenched her hands into fists. "Tell me the truth for once," she pleaded.

Dad's stiff posture relaxed into a slouched position of defeat. "I never meant for this to happen," he said. His voice faded into an apologetic silence. He didn't make eye contact with any of them.

"Are you in love with her?"

Dad nodded. "I'm staying in B.C. to be with her."

Sarah couldn't breathe. It was as if the air had been sucked out of her lungs.

"When were you going to tell me? You can't do this," Mom begged. "We can work this out. I can be better." Tears fell down her flushed cheeks.

"I never meant to hurt you, Alice." He took her face into his hands and wiped her tears away with his thumbs.

"Don't do this."

"It's over, Alice. I'm sorry."

"How can you say that?" Her voice was fragile and shaking. "We have two children together. How could you do this to our family?"

Without answering, Dad went back into the bedroom. Mom didn't move. Minutes seemed like an eternity. When he finally returned, he had his suitcase in hand. His head hung low.

"Girls, I will call you soon." And with that, Dad walked out the front door and out of their lives. Mom ran to her bedroom. Sarah and Mabel followed. Their mom's gut-wrenching sobs were muffled by her pillow. Her white cotton pillowcase became soaked in her tears. It crushed Sarah to see her mother's frail body curled up on the bed in the fetal position. Pete whined and paced the bedroom floor. Sarah reached for Mabel's hand, but Mabel pulled away.

"You just let him leave?" Mabel screamed at their mother.

"Come on, Mabel, that's not fair." Sarah placed her hand on Mabel's shoulder, but she shrugged her off.

"This is all your fault," Mabel said, pointing her finger at Mom.

Their mother sat up in the bed and wiped her puffy, bloodshot eyes.

"Mabel, I—"

But before she could finish, Mabel fled the room and slammed the door behind her.

Mom opened her arms to Sarah. "It's okay. Come here."

Sarah collapsed into the safety of her mother's arms. The dam broke. As the tears burst and spilled down Sarah's cheeks, Mom held her tightly and gently rocked her back and forth just like she had when Sarah was a baby. Her blonde hair fell in Sarah's face. It smelled clean, like Pantene.

"I'll never forgive him," said Sarah. "Never." She closed her eyes and let the waves of grief crash down on her. Exhausted, she allowed the undertow to pull her into a fitful sleep.

Sarah snapped wide awake an hour later. Her mouth felt like a dry cotton ball. Her mother had fallen asleep, too. Sarah was careful not to wake her as she slipped out of the spoon and onto the pine floors. Before she left, she took the throw from the end of the bed and pulled it over top of her mother.

Sarah still felt dehydrated after chugging two glasses of water at the kitchen sink. She filled her cup for a third time and went to check on Mabel. She knocked on her bedroom door. No answer. Sarah looked at the clock in the living area and remembered Mabel was scheduled to work the afternoon shift at the restaurant. Sarah wished her sister had called in sick. She was scared of being alone. She didn't know how to deal with these big feelings. Her hands began to shake. She chewed her thumbnail until the skin around it hurt. Breathing suddenly felt hard. Her chest grew tight as bile rose in her throat. She couldn't breathe. She needed air.

Sarah quickly opened the sliding glass door and stepped into the sunshine. The bright afternoon light launched an assault on her sore, sensitive eyes. She brought her hand to her forehead to shade her eyes from the painful light. The air was as thick and hot as soup. She took deep, long-drawn breaths and could feel the thudding in her chest begin to subside.

A dragonfly took a rest on her shoulder. He was all black, but his face was white. Sarah brought her nose close to his. He tilted his head and stared right back at her. He shimmied his shoulders and rubbed his hands together. They both soaked in the warmth of the sun on their backs. Sarah's grandmother had loved dragonflies.

She looked out across the bay and watched as a father and his two children jumped off a floating raft hand in hand. Watching the familiar scene unfold was like a kick to the stomach. She longed for those carefree days of her childhood when her parents were happy and her grandmother was still alive.

"Life is like a trail," her grandma had once said to her on one of their early morning hikes. "The path will be winding and sometimes lonesome." She stopped and admired the daisies among the tall, wild grass. She gently petted their silky white petals. "May yours lead to the most amazing view, Sarah."

If the death of her grandma had taught her anything, it was that life goes on. There was no going back.

ALYSSA DELLE PALME

Chapter Twelve

Sarah was sitting in a green Adirondack chair on the dock when she saw Jeff fishing in his kayak in the bay. When he saw her, he reeled in his line and paddled toward the shoreline.

"Where have you been all week?" he asked.

"Working," Sarah said in an emotionless tone.

Jeff's brow creased with concern. Sarah shifted uncomfortably in her chair. She knew how unkempt she looked. She didn't have the energy to brush her hair, and her eyes were permanently puffy from crying herself to sleep every night.

Jeff paddled his kayak into shallow water, swung his legs out of the boat, and stood up. He pulled his kayak onto the sand and hopped onto the dock. He knelt by Sarah's side and gave her knee a gentle shake. "I called on you a couple of times this week, but no one answered the door. Is everything okay?"

"No," said Sarah, her voice cracking. She blurted out the whole story about how her father had left. She told him about how her mother hadn't left her room all week and how Mabel had basically disappeared, only to return late at night to sleep before taking off again in the morning. "He couldn't even look at me when he said goodbye."

"What a prick," said Jeff.

Sarah curled into a ball. Her shoulders heaved as she sobbed quietly into her arms. Jeff didn't try to reassure her or fix the situation. He just stayed by her side and held space for her while she cried. Eventually, she poked her head up and wiped her runny nose on the cuff of her sweatshirt.

"I'm such a mess." She shivered. Despite it being

summer, Sarah felt like she couldn't keep warm.

"I'm worried about you. There's a party down the lake tonight, and I think you should come. Hugo is coming, and we're taking the motorboat. He could be just the distraction you need." Jeff wiggled his eyebrows, making Sarah crack a teensy smile.

"I don't know. I—"

"Just think about it." He stood up and gave her a quick peck on the cheek before pulling his kayak back into the water. "I've got to head back. I told my dad I'd help him stack firewood. I'll be around, though, so if you need anything, I'm here."

Sarah nodded and bit her lip to stop herself from crying again. All week, she had felt like she was lost and stumbling around in the dark. Jeff's kindness was the light she had desperately needed.

Sarah heaved herself out of her chair and forced her stiffened legs to climb the mountain of stairs back up to the cottage. Inside, she pulled a cucumber from the refrigerator and cut a couple of slices to put on her swollen eyes. As she lay in the darkness, Sarah felt the fear of being alone creep back in. She didn't want to go to the party, but decided it couldn't be worse than being isolated in her bedroom on another beautiful summer night.

A week of cathartic crying meant Sarah needed a full day of primping. She applied a thick and creamy face mask called *Beauty Sleep*. After tossing and turning all night, Sarah needed a face mask that promised to fake a little shut-eye. It left her skin feeling bouncy and restored. She shaved her legs, washed her hair, and tidied up her eyebrows by plucking a few stray hairs. She added two coats of an icy blue pearl polish to her toenails. Sarah emerged from the bathroom feeling renewed.

In her bedroom, Sarah dropped her towel and

slipped into a floral tunic dress. The breezy dress showed off her toned legs. She was never able to wear this dress at her high school. Her Catholic school had a rule that the bottom of a skirt could not be shorter than a girl's fingertips when she held her arms by her side.

Sarah once had a science teacher who loved to enforce the dress code. Mr. C was a short man with a receding hairline, and his breath smelled sour like plain yogurt. Rumor had it he walked up and down the rows of desks because he got off on looking down girls' blouses. One day, Julie had been wearing a sleeveless dress shirt, and her bra strap had slipped down her arm as she worked on an assignment. Mr. C walked by and lifted her bra strap up with the end of his yellow pencil.

"Your attire is not appropriate for school, Miss Lachance."

"It's not a tank top," Julie replied. Her face glowed red, and she fidgeted with her top button.

"Detention after school."

"But Mr. C, that's not fair. This is a Club Monaco dress shirt."

"I suggest you reread your student handbook, Miss Lachance. Bra straps are against the school's dress code. We don't want the boys to get distracted now, do we?"

Julie had sat with her elbows on her desk, chin in hands, and stared at her assignment. Sarah knew she was fighting back tears.

"The dress code is bullshit," Sarah called from the back of the room. Swearing was also against the school's policy, but she did it to protect Julie. She didn't want Julie to have to go to detention alone with Mr. Creep. "It's sexist."

"That's enough out of you, Miss Williams. It looks like I'll be seeing you after school for detention as well."

Julie turned around in her desk and smiled at Sarah. "Thank you," she mouthed silently.

Alone in her cottage bedroom, Sarah stood in front of her full-length mirror, missing her best friend more than ever. Julie was away at a performing arts workshop in Toronto for a couple of weeks, so Sarah hadn't been able to tell her what had happened yet.

Sarah grabbed her makeup bag and sat on the floor in front of the mirror. Her mother had bought her a beechwood vanity with a stool and a round mirror, but Sarah preferred to do her makeup on the floor. Her eyes were still tender and red from crying. She applied a dark, smokey eye to help cover up the puffiness.

"I wish you wouldn't wear so much makeup," her mother said when Sarah emerged from her room. "Your eyes are so big and beautiful. You don't need makeup."

Sarah felt crushed by her mom's criticism. Irritation stirred within her.

"I didn't ask for your opinion," Sarah snapped. "I'm wearing so much makeup to hide the fact that my eyes look like Sylvester Stallone's after fifteen rounds in Rocky." Sarah held back her tears as she picked up her purse and shoes. She refused to let the mascara that she had so carefully applied earlier run down her cheeks.

"I'm sorry, Sarah. I shouldn't have said anything. I didn't mean to—"

"I'll be home late, so don't wait up."

Anger gripped Sarah as she hurried outside and slammed the sliding glass door behind her. She instantly regretted leaving like that, but something was holding her back from going inside and apologizing to her mother. Sarah knew her father's abandonment wasn't her mother's fault, but she couldn't shake the anger that burned in her chest. She felt mad at the world. Sarah took a few deep breaths to compose herself and then took the shortcut through the pine grove to the Roberts' cottage.

The short walk under the canopy of trees helped Sarah pull herself together. The movement of time seemed to slow down as she listened to the soft breeze move through the branches above.

"I'm so glad you made it," Jeff said when Sarah emerged from the forest. He picked up the heavy cooler full of beer and cocked his head toward the dock. "Hugo is getting the boat ready. Let's go."

Sarah wasn't as nervous to see Hugo as she thought she would be. Even the butterflies that had fluttered in her stomach whenever Hugo was around seemed to have migrated to Mexico early. Hugo welcomed her aboard and flashed his irritatingly handsome smile, but Sarah felt indifferent. Detached. It was as if the chemistry they had shared earlier in the summer had fallen flat. She had the sudden urge to jump off the boat and retreat to her bedroom.

"I've missed you, beautiful," said Hugo. He squeezed her hand and led her to the bench chaise lounge that wrapped around the front of the boat. "I'm the captain tonight. Can I get you a drink before we head out?"

Sarah managed to slap a smile on her face and nodded.

"I'll grab you a Coke," he said. Hugo sat down in the captain's chair and opened the cooler.

"Actually, I'll take a beer."

"Really?" said Jeff, handing Hugo the lanyard to start the boat. Hugo turned on the ignition and slowly started driving the pontoon away from the dock and into the bay.

"I could use a drink," she said loudly over the motor.

Jeff grabbed a couple of beers and used his teeth to open the bottles. He handed one to Sarah and sat down on the bench beside her.

"Cheers to a great night!" he said.

Sarah chugged her beer until her throat burned and her belly bloated. Foam dripped down her chin.

"Woah, pace yourself."

Sarah wiped away her white mustache. "I'd like another, please."

By the time they arrived, Sarah had already polished off two bottles of beer. Hugo lugged the cooler onto the dock and headed toward the house. Jeff held Sarah's hand as she stumbled off the boat.

"This cottage is enormous," she said in awe. The cottage was like a mansion that sat on a beautiful, treed lot overlooking the lake. The private beach stretched for miles with hardly a neighbor in view. Sarah saw Hugo carry the cooler onto the porch that spanned the front of the property. People were scattered everywhere.

"The owner is a Member of Parliament," said Jeff. He guided Sarah to a wooden bench next to the raging campfire and parked her there. "Apparently, his ex-wife got the cottage in the divorce, and she likes to rub it in by hosting parties all summer. Rumor has it, she acquired all their mutual friends in the split, too. I mean, it would be difficult for anyone to turn down an invitation to a beautiful lake house."

At the mere mention of divorce, Sarah felt her throat tighten up. "So, we're at the party of an MP's pissed ex-wife?" she asked.

"No, we're at the party of an MP's pissed ex-wife's son. He got the keys for the weekend to celebrate his college graduation."

A guy with a ponytail sitting beside them at the campfire offered Jeff the joint he was smoking.

"Naw, man, thanks," said Jeff.

"Smoke?" the stranger asked Sarah.

Sarah had never smoked marijuana before. She had always been afraid of experimenting with drugs since taking the Substance Abuse unit in elementary school.

In grade six, Sarah's class was led to the library and seated in the carpeted pit for the lesson. A local police officer had set up a projector to show the kids the horrors of methamphetamine.

"This is a woman before using meth," the officer had said, showing the prepubescent children a photograph of a friendly looking lady. He changed the slide. "This is that same woman after using meth."

Sarah had been horrified. The woman's face was covered in small sores, and most of her teeth had fallen out. The ones that remained were black with decay from the harsh chemicals of the drugs. The young woman also looked like she had aged 50 years. The officer went on to explain to the class that marijuana was "the gateway drug." Ever since, Sarah had turned down any offer to smoke pot.

The guy with the ponytail held the skunky blunt out to Sarah. She took the white joint between her fingers and inhaled. The nausea she had been feeling earlier suddenly dissipated. She took another toke.

"Okay, I think that's enough," said Jeff. He took the joint from Sarah and gave it back to the guy with the ponytail. "I didn't know you smoked weed," he said to Sarah.

Sarah held her breath until her throat tickled, making her cough a white cloud of smoke. "I don't." Sarah smiled. She felt euphoric. "But I've been missing out!" Sarah tried to stand up, but the weed made her lightheaded.

"Easy," said Jeff. "Maybe we should sit by the

fire for a while. When Hugo gets back, I'll get him to grab you a bite to eat.

Sarah started giggling. "I'm so hungry!" She lifted her legs onto the bench and laid her head in Jeff's lap. The world was spinning. "Jeff, you're the best friend a girl could ever have."

Jeff laughed. "I think someone is having a good night."

Sarah nodded. They sat quietly for a while, watching the fire dance.

"Jeff, can I tell you a secret?" she asked. When Jeff leaned his ear down, she whispered, "I'm in love with your brother."

"Ha! You're officially intoxicated."

Sarah sat up sharply and took Jeff's hands in hers. "No, really, I love Scott, and I don't know what to do about it."

"Sarah, Scott can be an asshole when it comes to—"

"I think about him all the time, Jeff. When we're at work, I catch myself staring at him and imagining what it would be like to be his girlfriend."

"Sarah—"

"Time flies whenever we're together and—"

"Sarah!" Jeff cut her off. "What about Hugo?"

Sarah's hands flew to her temples. In her high haze, she had forgotten about Hugo.

"Where is he anyway?" Sarah said, looking around the party.

"I'm not sure." Jeff stood up and did a 360. "I thought you liked him."

"I did. I mean, I do." Sarah cupped her chin in her hands and massaged her temples. Her mouth suddenly felt like a hot towel straight out of the dryer. Her saliva was thick and stringy. "I'm so thirsty."

"Side effect of the weed. I'll go get you some water." Jeff patted her on the back and headed toward the cottage.

Moments later, someone passed her a dripping can of beer. Without even thanking the stranger, Sarah grabbed the cold drink and downed it in five gulps.

"Slow down, chickee." Kurt slumped into the blue plastic Muskoka chair beside her and rubbed his blond goatee, still greasy, but with food caught in it. He undressed her with his perverted eyes. Sarah crushed her beer can and belched. Her eyes widened, and she quickly covered her mouth with her hand. When Sarah was younger, her grandma would make her say, "Excuse me for my indiscretion," any time a little burp escaped her lips at the dinner table.

"Kurt, excuse me for my indiscretion." Sarah burst into a fit of giggles.

Kurt leaned forward. "I think it's pretty hot when a woman can burp like a lumberjack." He licked the cold sore in the corner of his chapped lips.

Sarah's shoulders shook so hard she doubled over.

"Sarah, are you okay?" Jeff said, standing there with a bottle of water and a bag of chips.

Sarah grabbed the collar of Jeff's shirt and pulled him down until his face was inches from her. "This is my boss, and he thinks my burps are sexy," she whispered. Sarah howled and repeatedly slapped her hand against the bench.

"All right, it's time to get you home." Jeff lifted Sarah's arm around his shoulders and slipped his arm around her waist. She waved to Kurt like the queen as Jeff dragged her toward the boat.

"Wait," said Sarah, digging her heels into the earth. "I'm going to pee my pants." She slipped out from under Jeff's grasp and ran for the trees to relieve herself.

It was sobering to step into the dark shadows. Sarah walked a little deeper into the forest for some privacy, but the tiny hairs on the back of her neck warned her that she wasn't alone. A twig snapped nearby, making Sarah jump. She placed her hand against the thick bark of a grandmother pine to steady herself. She waited for her eyes to adjust to the dark. Under the light of the moon, Sarah could make out two figures hooking up against another tree. Her jaw dropped when she realized she had stumbled upon Hugo and Shannon.

Chapter Thirteen

"You asshole!" Sarah yelled, watching Hugo slip his hand up Shannon's shirt. Her high-pitched scream startled the couple, and Shannon quickly pulled down her blouse.

"Sarah?" said Hugo. "I'm sorry. I—"

"I thought you said she wasn't your girlfriend," Shannon whispered harshly, tucking her shirt back into her jeans.

How could he have done this to me? Sarah stood there with her hands clenched by her side, breathless with anger. Hugo took a step toward her.

"Sarah, it was a mistake—"

Sarah squeezed her eyes shut and brought her hands to her ears to block him out. She had reached the end of her rope. "Shut up!" she screamed. Hugo raised his hands and backed off. Sarah opened her eyes and wagged her finger at him. Her whole hand shook with fury. "The mistake was all mine, Hugo, for ever having trusted you."

Sarah took off running deeper into the forest.

Guys are all the same, she thought. *Cheating scumbags.*

Hugo's pleas for her to come back only made her run away faster. Short, thorny plants scraped Sarah's bare legs until they bled, but she kept on running. She was desperate to escape. Blinded by darkness and tears, Sarah tripped over a large tree root sticking out of the ground and landed on all fours. She scraped both knees in the fall, and tiny pebbles stuck to the palms of her hands. She hung her head low and sobbed. When she was able to catch her breath, Sarah slowly picked herself up and hobbled the rest of her way out of the forest. Once she reached the dirt road, she saw a pair of headlights driving toward her and she stuck out her thumb. She would hitchhike her way back home. As the black truck pulled to the side of the road, Sarah remembered the promise she had made to her parents about never hitchhiking. Her mother's voice warning her she could be murdered rang in her ears as the driver of the black truck rolled down his passenger side window.

"Sarah? What the hell are you doing?" Scott asked.

Sarah pressed her hands to her heart and let out a huge sigh of relief. She wouldn't die at the hands of a stranger tonight. "I need a ride."

"Get in."

Sarah climbed into Scott's truck, put on her seatbelt, and stared straight ahead.

"Jesus, what happened to you?" Scott reached across the armrest console and pulled a twig out of Sarah's hair.

"I don't want to talk about it."

Scott looked down at Sarah's scraped and bruised knees. "Did somebody hurt you?"

Sarah shook her head. "No, nothing like that."

"Do you want me to take you home?"

Sarah swallowed. Her throat felt sore and rough like sandpaper. Smoking marijuana at the party had irritated her throat. It burned when she swallowed, and she still felt tipsy from the beer and weed.

"Scott, could we go for a drive?" The thought of going back to the cottage where her father was no longer staying with them made Sarah's stomach churn.

"You bet. I'll take you to my favorite place."

Sarah relaxed into the soft leather of the passenger

seat, closed her eyes, and listened to the new album by The Cranberries that Scott had playing on his radio. She opened her eyes again when she felt Scott put the truck into park. "Where are we?"

"The lookout." Scott opened his door and hopped out of the truck. Sarah thought he looked cute in his relaxed-fit jeans and gray hoodie. Scott walked around to the back of the truck and grabbed something from the bed before opening Sarah's passenger side door.

"Turn and face me," he said, placing his first aid kit on the floor of the truck. After Sarah did as she was told, Scott tore a small white wrapper with his teeth and gently cleaned Sarah's scrapes with an antiseptic wipe.

"Ouch! That stings!"

Scott softly blew onto her open cuts, taking away the burning sensation. "Better?"

Sarah nodded. She couldn't take her eyes off him as he grabbed a tube of Polysporin and applied the antibiotic cream to her cuts. He placed a Band-Aid on each knee to protect the bigger scrapes.

When he was finished, Scott grabbed her hand and pulled her out of the truck. "Close your eyes." Scott slowly started walking, leading her by the hand.

"Where are you taking me?" Sarah tried to peek, but Scott caught her in the act and came around behind her. He placed his hands over her eyes. "No peeking," he whispered in her ear.

Sarah was convinced Scott could feel her heart hammering in her chest as they walked in silence. She took small steps and held her arms out in front of her, afraid she would get hit in the face by a branch.

"Wait here a second," he said. Sarah heard some movement and moments later, Scott took both her hands into his. "It's a big step."

"Scott, I'm scared."

"You can trust me, Sarah."

Sarah thought about all the times Scott had stuck by her side. He had never left her when they played capture the flag in the forest at night, and he had stayed with her the entire time they had swum to the raft in the pitch black. Sarah took a deep breath and squeezed her eyes shut, stepping up to meet Scott wherever he was because she trusted him.

He didn't let her hands go. "Open your eyes."

The happy tickle in Sarah's chest exploded when she saw the view. They were standing on a retaining wall made of stone at the top of an escarpment. The bright light of the moon reflected in the lake below.

"The moon changes constantly," her grandma had told Sarah the summer she was nine. At that age, Sarah had been curious about all things space related, so her grandma took the time to teach her about the different phases of the moon. Throughout July and August, they tracked the moon's waning and waxing stages.

One night, Sarah ran inside the cottage screaming with excitement, "Grandma! The moon is a waxing gibbous!" All the adults had erupted in laughter.

Sarah swallowed back tears as she watched the silver moonbeam glisten in the gentle waves below. Her life felt like it was waning. Her father had left, and Hugo was now with Shannon, but thinking about her grandma reminded Sarah that this was just a phase. Like the moon, she would be whole again soon.

"I've never taken anyone here before," Scott said, squeezing Sarah's hand. The moonlight illuminated his handsome face against the velvety green backdrop of the forest behind him. A barred owl hooted nearby. Sarah could tell by its distinct call, like it was saying *Who cooks for you? Who cooks for you-all?*

Sarah freed her hand from Scott's and sat down

on the retaining wall. She began kicking her feet against the solid stones. "You were right about Hugo."

Scott sat down next to Sarah, shoulder to shoulder.

"I found him hooking up with Shannon in the woods."

Scott clenched his jaw. "That piece of shit. I'm going to—"

"No! You're not going to do anything. I don't even know how I feel about the whole situation yet."

"He'll just do it to you again, Sarah."

Sarah shook her head. "That's not what I meant. When I saw them kissing, it was like I didn't even care. Sure, it bruised my ego a bit, but I was more upset that he was lying about it. That he was sneaking around. He's two-faced, just like—"

"Your dad?"

"How did you know? Did Jeff...?"

"I wasn't supposed to say anything. Please don't be mad at Jeff. He had to tell us. My mom was on her way over to your cottage to invite your parents for a barbeque. Jeff wanted to save your mom the embarrassment."

"My life is like an episode of *Days of our Lives.*" Sarah covered her face with her hands.

Scott wrapped his arm around Sarah's shoulders. "Have you confronted your dad?"

Sarah shook head. "He's called a couple of times, but I can't bring myself to talk to him. I'm just so pissed off right now."

"What if you wrote it all down in one of those notebooks you're always carrying around? It might be a good way for you to process how you're feeling and how you might approach talking to your dad."

Sarah pursed her lips together. "Something to

think about." She leaned her head against Scott's shoulder. "I'm sorry I ruined your night."

"You didn't ruin it. It's probably better I didn't go to the party. Right about now, I'd probably be suffering the wrath of Britney."

"Trouble in paradise?"

"I broke things off with her. I knew she had feelings for me. I should've never started things back up with her in the first place."

"Then why did you?"

Scott shrugged his shoulders. "I was lonely and selfish, I guess. Besides, I like someone else." Scott's eyes clung to hers.

For a brief moment, Sarah thought that maybe he was talking about her. Seconds later, she reminded herself that he only saw her as a friend. Sarah looked away, struggling with how she felt to hear him say that he had feelings for someone else. She was curious to know who he was talking about, but she wasn't ready to talk about his love life. Especially when hers was in shambles. Sarah cleared her throat and met his gaze. "I'm swearing off guys. You're all trouble."

"I'm swearing off women, too. Most of them anyway."

"Ha! I'd like to see you try."

"I'm serious, Sarah. I'm ready for a relationship with someone special. I'm tired of dating around. I want something real."

Sarah imagined for a moment that this was it, the moment he was going to ask her to be his girlfriend. She drummed her feet against the smooth stone wall to the beat of her own heart.

"I know, I sound like a loser," Scott said.

Sarah lifted her head off his shoulder and looked him square in the face. "Not at all. Actually, I think it's the sweetest thing I've ever heard you say."

Scott looked up at the moon. "Since we've both sworn off dating, maybe we could spend more time hanging out this summer," he said.

"I would like that very much."

"All the fun without the pressure to be anyone else but me. I feel like I can be myself around you, Sarah." He stood up on the retaining wall and held out his hand. "I want to show you something else."

Sarah accepted his hand and followed Scott behind his truck. He opened the tailgate and placed his hands around her waist. "Jump," he instructed, lifting her onto the lip of his pickup before hopping in behind her.

He handed Sarah a couple of pillows. She watched as he pulled a sleeping bag from its stuff sack and unrolled it in the bed of his truck. Sarah passed him the pillows, and Scott fluffed them up before laying them down inside the sleeping bag. Scott rested his head on one pillow and patted the open space next to him. "Come lie with me."

The tickle inside Sarah's chest jumped into her throat. She wiped her clammy palms on her dress and slipped inside the sleeping bag next to Scott. The fleece inside the bag felt soft against her exposed skin. The night air was warm, but Sarah shivered. She pulled the sleeping bag up to her chin. Her brain had just sworn off men, but her heart told her that wasn't true. She liked the way her body felt next to his. For the first time in a while, Sarah felt safe. She shuddered with pleasure as Scott's hand accidentally brushed against the outside of her thigh.

He lifted his hand and pointed to the sky. "Do you see those five bright stars?"

Sarah pulled her gaze away from his handsome face and looked up. A rich section of the Milky Way was painted across the night sky like white paint splattered against a black canvas. Sarah snuggled in closer to Scott to see which stars he was pointing at. Sarah followed his index finger as he traced a "W" in the sky.

"That's Cassiopeia. It's my favorite constellation," he said.

"Why is that?"

"Because it reminds me of you." Scott turned onto his side and traced the tiny freckles on Sarah's nose.

Sarah closed her eyes and luxuriated in his gentle caress.

Scott rolled onto his back and opened his arm, inviting Sarah in again. Her heart leapt in response. She settled in, enjoying the feel of him. When he wrapped his arm around her shoulders, she cuddled into the nook against his chest. His curly hair was splayed about the pillow, and his lips were slightly parted. She had longed to kiss those full lips for as long as she could remember. She listened to the strong beat of his heart.

"You're going to be okay, Sarah."

"How can you be so sure?"

"I know you're in a really dark place right now, but just look up." Scott waved his free hand across the sky. "The darkest of nights give us the brightest stars."

Sarah traced Cassiopeia with her eyes until she drifted off in Scott's arms. She was relaxed for the first time since her dad had left, and content, maybe more content than she remembered ever feeling. Sarah knew deep down that even the stars couldn't shine without the darkness … and then she was asleep.

Chapter Fourteen

"Sarah," Scott whispered in her ear. "I should take you home. It's late and your mom will worry."

Sarah opened her eyes and blinked. It took her a moment to get her bearings in the dark. When she realized she wasn't dreaming, she groaned. She didn't want to leave the comfort of Scott's arms or the warmth of the sleeping bag. "What time is it?"

"2:00 in the morning."

Sarah sat upright with a jolt. "My mom probably thinks I'm dead in a ditch somewhere!"

The drive back to the cottage was quiet. Sarah's head was pounding, the terrible aftereffects of too much partying. She wanted to know what Scott was thinking and feeling, but it was too hard to focus with a hangover. When Scott pulled up to the Williams' driveway, he turned off his headlights. Sarah was relieved to see the cottage was dark. Her mother was asleep.

Sarah hesitated before getting out of the truck, hoping Scott would say something, but he stared straight ahead. Disappointed, she unbuckled her seatbelt and opened the door. "Thanks for everything, Scott. I really appreciate what you did for me tonight."

Scott smiled and tipped his head. A hint of desire showed in his green eyes. "Of course. That's what friends are for. I'll let Jeff and Hugo know you got home okay, too."

Sarah swallowed hard. She forced a smile and shut the truck door as quietly as she could. She squared her shoulders and began walking toward the cottage.

"Sarah!" Scott whispered loudly out his open window.

Sarah turned expectantly. "Yes?"

"Call your dad. Let him know how you're feeling. It might make you feel better."

It wasn't what she was hoping Scott would say, but it felt good to have him looking out for her. "Okay. I will."

The next day, before she could change her mind, Sarah picked up the beige phone in the kitchen and quickly punched in her father's number. She had decided to take Scott's advice and had spent the morning journaling her thoughts and feelings. She wasn't sure what she was going to say to her dad, but despite his betrayal, Sarah loved him and wanted her dad in her life.

"Allo?" answered a woman with a French accent. Her voice was hoarse like a two-pack-a-day smoker.

Sarah shook with fury. She slammed the phone down. Resentment clouded her thoughts. She reached for the phone and hit the redial button. She yearned to give that woman a piece of her mind, but this time, her father answered.

"Hello?"

"Dad?" Sarah's voice was barely audible. She felt as if she were choking on her rage.

"Sarah?"

"Was that her?" Sarah spit the words out in disgust. It felt as if she had a hair stuck to her tongue.

"Yes. Her name is Emilee. I'd like you to meet her."

Sarah bit her lip in an attempt to control her anger. She had promised herself she wouldn't cry on the phone. Her bottom lip, clenched between her teeth like a bear trap, thumped in pain. When she finally released it, Sarah could taste pennies on the tip of her tongue.

"Sarah, I never meant for anyone to get hurt."

"How could you do this to our family?"

"The problems between your mother and I have nothing to do with you."

"How could you leave me?" Sarah sank to the floor with the phone cradled between her ear and shoulder. She began to weep.

"Please don't cry. I love you, Sarah—"

"Pay her no attention. That's what she wants," Emilee said in the background. "She'll come around. Come back to bed."

Sarah uncurled her body off the ground and slowly stood up. "I'll never forgive you."

"Sarah, wait—"

But she didn't. She had heard enough. Her father had made his choice. Sarah hung up the phone and wiped away her tears. She jumped when the phone rang moments later.

"Sarah!" her mother called from the deck outside. "Can you answer the phone?"

Sarah didn't budge. When the phone kept ringing, her mother came inside.

"What's the matter? Why won't you answer?" Her mother gave Sarah a concerned look as she picked up the receiver. "Hello?"

Sarah cringed as she watched her become flustered. Sarah knew her mother wasn't expecting to hear her father's voice on the other end.

"Jack! Hi, I—"

Silence followed as her mother listened to what he had to say.

"What shitty thing did I just do?" Mom guffawed. "I didn't put her up to anything!"

Sarah couldn't hear what her father was saying, but she knew he was reaming her mother out. Sarah's stomach knotted at the thought of causing her mom more pain.

"I'm not playing stupid, Jack. I don't know what you're talking about. I was—"

Mom's face darkened with a deeply sad expression. She slowly replaced the phone in the receiver. "He hung up on me."

Sarah lowered her head. Guilt clutched at her heart.

"What did you say to your father?"

Sarah shrugged. Her senses were spinning.

Mom placed both hands on Sarah's shoulders and gave them a gentle shake. "Talk to me," she pleaded.

"I confronted him. I asked him how he could leave me," Sarah said, her voice cracking. "I told him I'd never forgive him."

"Oh, honey." Her mother pulled her close and wrapped her arms around her tightly. They swayed in an embrace for a while, a silent slow dance of love and support for one another. They could have spent their entire day analyzing the situation over and over again. They could have brainstormed ideas on how to put the pieces of their life back together, but instead, they left the pieces where they lay and moved on with their day.

Sarah's grandma said the lake was a place to heal. Sarah changed into her bikini and went for a swim. As she dove underwater, the negative feelings she had experienced that morning started to wash away. When her head emerged from the lake, she felt cleansed of her worries. The wild air was rejuvenating. Though her conversation with her dad hadn't gone the way she had hoped, it felt good to be honest with him. Scott was right. It was empowering to use her voice.

Sarah swam across the bay to the Draper's cottage and touched their dock before turning around. Her wet handprint embedded in the wood but would soon disappear under the sun's rays.

"They'll think mermaids were here," Mabel had whispered one summer afternoon when they were younger. They had both placed a wet handprint on the Draper's dock. The goal of their game was not to get caught, for it would ruin the magic of the mermaids. They had permission to swim across the small bay as long as they wore their lifejackets. Sarah and Mabel imagined the bay was a mermaid lagoon, and they were the fairies of the sea. They would cross their ankles and pretend they were swimming with green fins. Sometimes, when Sarah knew her mother was distracted by a good book, Sarah would take her lifejacket off and dive down to grab a few pieces of seaweed for their hair.

Mr. and Mrs. Draper were in their eighties now and had moved into a retirement home in the city a few years back. Their cottage had stood vacant ever since. Sarah treaded water and waited for her magical mermaid print to disappear before swimming back.

For old time's sake, Sarah crossed her ankles and pushed the water up and down with her make-believe fin. It was a lot harder than she remembered. When she reached the raft, she hauled herself out and lay down on the hot, dry wood. Sarah listened to the whisper-song of a blue jay. She knew all the notes by heart. The collection of whirrs, clicks, and whines.

"Blue jays are bullies," her grandma had told her once when she was younger. "They plunder other birds' nests."

"But they're so beautiful!"

Sarah loved their distinctive blue wings and black necklace. As a child, she was determined to find a blue jay feather for her collection, which consisted mostly of feathers from wild turkeys. Turkey feathers were easy to find because they lost a lot of them during their molting period. Her grandma believed finding a feather in your path was a blessing.

The blue jay's song faded away. Sarah rotated herself on the raft like a rotisserie chicken. The sun sizzled the droplets on her back.

In the distance, Hugo ran down the stairs to the Roberts' dock. He cannonballed into the lake and freestyled toward her like an Olympic gold medalist. Sarah gasped and tucked her face into her arms, desperate to camouflage her body against the raft. Her mind frantically tried to replay everything she had said to him at the party, but that part of the evening was still hazy. Moments later, the raft rocked like a sailboat at sea as Hugo pulled himself out of the lake.

"I need to talk to you," he said breathlessly.

"Go away, Hugo," she murmured from the safety of her arm cave. She promised herself she would never drink again. The hangover guilt was awful.

"You were right about what you said last night. I am an asshole."

Sarah peaked one eye out from underneath her arm. Hugo sat beside her with one foot on the raft and the other dangling in the lake, sunning himself like the *Le Faune Barberini* sculpture minus the exposed penis. Hugo's muscular body was like a replica of the famous marble statue that Sarah had studied in her high school art history class.

"What I did to you was wrong, Sarah. I'm sorry for hurting you."

Sarah turned her head toward Hugo and used her arm as a pillow. "I'm sorry, too."

"What do you have to be sorry about? You've been nothing but—"

"I drank too much last night and acted hysterical. I should've never run off like that."

"You were upset."

Sarah nodded. "But you were honest with me, that day on the dock. You told me to my face that you weren't looking for anything serious. You said you wanted to have fun, and if I'm being totally honest, too, I know I haven't been a whole lot of fun lately."

"Do you want to talk about it?"

Sarah shook her head. She was done talking about her father.

Hugo smiled and squeezed her arm. "Friends?"

"Definitely."

Suddenly, Hugo's smile fell from his face. His golden complexion turned gray like the clay they sometimes had found at the bottom of the lake when they were kids.

"Sarah, don't move."

Her whole body stiffened and froze to the raft. She felt a tickle on her calf and whipped her head around to see a huge furry brown spider running up her leg.

"Dock spider!" she screamed. Sarah's body thawed enough for her to jump to her feet and try to shake it off. She smacked the back of her legs before jumping into the lake as if she was on fire. Hugo leapt in after her.

"That thing looked like a tarantula!" Hugo said once they swam a safe distance from the raft.

Sarah circled her legs like an eggbeater to tread water. "I hate them. They give me the heebie-jeebies."

"The heebie what?"

Sarah laughed. She wondered what the Swiss-German translation was for that word. "Spiders creep me out."

"Me, too. That thing was the size of my hand!"

"They're the biggest spiders in Canada."

"Are they venomous?"

"No. They don't even bite. I don't know why I'm

so afraid of them."

When they were younger, Sarah, Mabel, Scott, and Jeff would bring a flip-flop with them when they'd swim to the raft to play four corners. Each of them stood at the edge of their own corner and bounced until someone lost their balance. One by one, they would fall into the lake. Last person standing was declared King of the Raft. Every now and then, when they'd bounce on the raft, water would splash between the cracks of the wood, and baby dock spiders would come running out. Whoever was closest to the spider would grab the flip-flop and slap the spider as hard as they could. Its guts splattered against the raft like a fly on a windshield. Sarah was never brave enough to pick up the flip-flop. She always froze at the sight of the spider. The others would yell at her to kill it, but she could only ever hear her heartbeat thumping in her ears. Someone else always had to grab the flip-flop and save her from an early demise.

"Sarah?" Hugo asked, waving his hand and bringing her back to the present.

Sarah gave her head a shake. "Sorry, Hugo, what did you say?"

"I said I have to get back. Jeff and I need to train for tryouts."

"Of course! I'll see you around, Hugo."

"I'm glad we talked."

"Me, too."

Sarah smiled as she watched Hugo swim back to the Roberts' dock. There was something about their breakup that made her feel mature, like an adult.

After her swim, Sarah wrapped a multi-striped Hudson's Bay towel around her waist and pulled an Adirondack chair out of the shade and into the sunshine. Someone on the lake was having a barbeque. The delicious smell of grilled meat and smokey sauce made

Sarah's stomach growl. The swim had made her hungry.

"Sarah!" Scott called from the landing at the top of the Williams' stairs. Sarah covered her eyes like a visor and waved hello. "What are you doing here?"

"Hugo told me I'd find you here." Scott grabbed the other Adirondack chair from the shade and pulled it next to Sarah. He leaned over and handed Sarah a textbook. She breathed him in. He smelled of sun and pine with a hint of lake water.

"For me?" she asked.

"Actually, it's for Mabel. I was at Fiddleheads with the guys the other night, and she was waiting on our table. I gave her a ride back after her shift, and she saw the book on my seat." Scott shrugged. "She seemed interested in the class and asked me to bring it over when I was finished with it."

Sarah knew that Mabel was interested in much more than a book. Her stomach churned. "I think she's home if you want to bring it up to her."

"Actually, I wanted to talk to you, and I thought you could give it to her for me." Scott reached for the book. "If it's a big deal, though, I can—"

"No, it's not a big deal." Sarah gripped the book tightly. "I'd be happy to give it to her for you." The familiar tickle in her heart bounced around her chest like a firefly trapped in a mason jar. It begged to be set free. "What did you want to talk to me about?"

"Well, I thought last night was pretty incredible, and I was wondering if you'd be up for another adventure with me."

A slow smile spread across Sarah's face. "What did you have in mind?"

"You'll have to wait and see."

"Come on! Why the secrecy?"

"When's your next day off?" he asked.

"Friday."

"Perfect, me, too." Scott hopped up and walked toward the stairs.

"I'll see you at work tomorrow," she called after him.

Sarah was giddy with excitement. She sank deeper into her chair and covered her ear-to-ear smile with her hand. She couldn't wait to spend an entire day with Scott, alone. She ignored the nervous thoughts that tried to swoop in and create chaos in her mind. She refused to think about the logistics of their situation anymore. Analyzing her feelings all the time was exhausting. She knew she was in love with Scott. She knew she wanted to be with him. She wondered what Scott had planned for Friday. Her imagination ran wild as she thought up all the different adventures they could go on—a road trip to a music festival or an outdoor picnic at a beach or maybe skinny dipping under the stars...

Sarah's stomach growled intensely, interrupting her daydream. She decided she would go upstairs, make a snack, and pick out the perfect outfit to wear on Friday. As she walked barefoot up the stairs to the cottage, she noticed a small blue jay feather in her path. Its beautiful blue hue stood out from the wooden stairs. Sarah picked up the feather in disbelief. It tickled the tips of her fingers. As she climbed the rest of the stairs, Sarah knew with her whole heart that this was a sign from her grandmother that she was on the right path.

Chapter Fifteen

Sarah couldn't concentrate at work. She sat in the tall lifeguard chair on the beach, scanning the lake for any swimmers in distress before she snuck another glance at Scott. To her delight, Scott was already staring back at her. Their eyes locked for a moment so intense it left Sarah breathless. The sound of a whistle snapped their spell. It was time to rotate positions. Sarah picked up her red torpedo and waited for Britney to take her place. She wasn't surprised when Britney snubbed her as she climbed down the lifeguard tower. Sarah jogged over to the First Aid station.

Inside, Shannon was sitting on a chair opposite a small boy and his worried mother. "That should do it," said Shannon. She gently placed a Flintstone Band-Aid across the boy's knee. Shannon invited the little boy to choose a sticker from the treasure box before he ventured back to the beach with his mother. Shannon scribbled her signature on the incident report and handed the clipboard to Sarah. "The First Aid kit needs to be restocked."

Sarah nodded. She took the form to the filing cabinet and slipped it into the accident reports folder.

"Sarah, listen, I—"

"There's no need to explain, Shannon. Hugo and I are just friends." Sarah was desperate to avoid this unnecessary and awkward conversation. Sarah and Shannon were not friends. No explanation needed. To avoid talking to Shannon, Sarah began organizing the forms in the filing cabinet in chronological order. She refused to fuel Shannon's mean girl burn. Sarah knew that Shannon had executed her plan to seduce Hugo with precise calculation in order to inflict havoc on Sarah. Sarah's high school had been full of backstabbing Shannon-types that thrived on confrontations. Before arriving at work earlier that day, Sarah had already decided that she would remove herself from the line of fire. There was no point in fighting with her. Sarah knew that Shannon did what she did because of her own insecurities.

"It was a bitch move, and I'm sorry."

Sarah raised her eyebrows, but didn't look up from her paperwork. She knew if she starved Shannon of the attention she craved, she would go prey on someone else. Shannon stood awkwardly at the door for a few moments, shifting her weight between her feet. When Sarah didn't take the bait, Shannon stormed off, cursing Sarah under her breath.

By the time the next whistle blew, signaling another rotation, Sarah had organized the entire filing cabinet. Pleased with her work, Sarah grabbed her red torpedo and was heading for the door when Scott stepped into the frame, blocking her exit.

"Hey there," he said, his voice rich and full of confidence.

They were standing so close their noses were almost touching. Scott smelled earthy, a perfect blend of sand and pine.

"What are you doing after work?" he asked.

Sarah shrugged. "I don't have any plans."

"I was thinking of heading to the lookout. I packed a couple of sandwiches and drinks. Do you want to come with me?"

Sarah bubbled inside with excitement. She blurted out an enthusiastic "yes" before scolding herself for answering so quickly. She didn't want to come across as desperate.

Scott laughed. "Great."

Sarah loved hearing his throaty chuckle. It warmed her insides like a sweet afternoon tea. Scott lingered in the door frame, smiling down at her.

"Scott, I have to get to my next rotation."

He shook his messy curls and stepped aside. "Right. Sorry."

Sarah grinned ear to ear as she jogged toward the beach to take her place in the lifeguard chair.

"Took you long enough," Britney sneered as she came down the tower. "What do you have to be so happy about?" Negativity oozed out of Britney's pores like an erupting pimple.

Sarah pushed past her and climbed to the top of the tower. "It's a beautiful day!" she declared.

After work, Sarah and Scott spent the rest of their afternoon relaxing at the lookout. The view looked different in the daytime. The yellow light from the sun bounced off the lake in a dazzling way. The forest surrounding the water was flourishing with many types of trees, plants, and animals. Captivating clouds slid across the blue sky while the lake below was busy with boaters. The energy of summer was in full swing.

Scott laid out a red and white checkered picnic blanket on the stone wall for them to sit on. He had packed a couple of ham and cheese sandwiches, a bag of plain potato chips, and two glass bottles of Coke. While they ate, they shared their thoughts on world views and talked about their favorite books and movies. Sarah loved how Scott's eyes twinkled with passion as he discussed his dreams of becoming a teacher up north in the Yukon one day.

"Teacher retention and turnover are big challenges for northern schools," he said. "I want to go where I'm needed."

"Do you think you'll miss city life?" Sarah asked.

"I don't want to live in the city. I like the comfort of a small community. I want my class to have access to the outdoors."

When it was her turn to share, Sarah appreciated how his eyebrows jumped with interest when she was explaining her writing project.

"I've almost finished drafting my first novel. It's a coming-of-age love story about a young girl and the boy who lives next door. It's set in the summer in a sleepy cottage town."

"You're really doing it, Sarah. I admire your dedication." The awe of his smile echoed in his voice.

Conversational sparks flew as they continued discussing different topics and ideas. There were never awkward lulls. It was the most invigorating conversation Sarah had had with someone in a long time.

The sun was setting by the time Scott dropped Sarah off at her cottage.

"See you Friday!" he said before driving away.

Sarah waved goodbye. Both her stomach and heart felt full and happy.

"Where were you?" her mother asked when Sarah waltzed through the front door. "You missed dinner."

Her mother was sitting on the couch, wrapped in a blanket with a glass of red wine in hand. Her hair was greasy, and her eyes were bloodshot. Sarah could tell she had been crying again.

"I went to the lookout with Scott after work."

"The lookout?"

"It's Scott's secret spot. It has the most spectacular views of the lake."

Her mother gave her a small knowing smile. "I'm glad you had a nice time, honey." She dragged herself off the couch and gave Sarah a quick peck on the cheek. "I'm going to go to bed. There are leftovers in the fridge. Mabel brought a lemon meringue pie home from work, too."

Sarah wasn't hungry, but she was enticed at the mention of dessert. She opened the fridge and took out the billowy pie and placed it on the counter. She grabbed a dessert fork and took a polite bite of bright yellow curd straight from the pie plate. She closed her eyes and hummed. The creamy filling was a perfect balance between sweet and tart. When she opened her eyes, she was surprised to see Mabel standing at the counter.

"You caught me red-handed," said Sarah. She sheepishly placed her fork in the sink and tiptoed with the pie back to the fridge.

"Scott took you to a lookout?" Mabel asked. Her tone was frigid.

Sarah's shoulders came crashing down. Mabel had overheard Sarah's conversation with their mother. There was no way out of this.

Mabel crossed her arms. "I thought you and Scott were just friends."

"We are. We—"

"Guys don't take their 'friends' to lookouts," she said, using air quotes. "I told you I was interested in him."

Sarah felt a flash of irritation and a sudden need to protect Scott. "You said you were interested in using him as a rebound." Sarah's words snapped through the air like a rubber band against a wrist.

"So what?" Mabel said, crossing her arms.

"Did you ever think about him and his feelings?"

"Trust me, I think Scott would be happy to—"

"No, he wouldn't! He's not like that."

"Ha! I bet a lot of women around this lake would beg to differ."

"Listen to what you're saying! Scott is your friend. You can't just use someone and then throw them away like a piece of trash. You're just like dad. I guess the apple doesn't fall far from the tree."

Mabel clenched her bottom lip between her teeth and looked away. As soon as Sarah had said it, she knew she had gone too far.

"Look Mabel, I—"

"You're a bitch."

As Mabel stormed off, a fresh swell of frustration rose in Sarah's chest. "He's not interested in you!" she called out.

Mabel slammed her bedroom door shut. Resentment smoldered in Sarah's body. She knew it had been a low blow comparing Mabel to their father, but at the same time, it was exhilarating to finally speak her mind. Sarah was tired of hiding behind halfhearted smiles to avoid confrontation. A heavy weight had lifted from her shoulders when she stood up to Mabel. It also gave her a boost of confidence, which was what she needed to finally tell Scott that she was in love with him.

On Friday afternoon, Sarah met Scott at the Roberts' dock. She still didn't know what adventure he had planned, but she wore her push-up bikini underneath her short jean cutoffs and yellow t-shirt just in case. Sarah's heart sank when she saw Scott packing small dry bags into the cargo compartment of his kayak.

When Sarah was younger, her grandmother had signed her and Mabel up for kayaking lessons at Pine Lake Beach. On the first day, the class was instructed to practice wet exits out of their kayaks. The male lifeguard with a curly rat-tail growing out the back of his zit-speckled neck flipped their kayaks one by one. Once submerged under water, they were told to push on the sides of their cockpit and let their lifejackets do the rest. When it came time for Sarah's turn, she told her instructor that she wasn't ready.

"Wet exits are an essential skill, Sarah. When it's

swimming time, you'll need to vamoose—"

The lifeguard flipped Sarah's kayak before she had a chance to take a breath. Water shot up her nose. She pushed against the sides of the cockpit, as she had been instructed to do, but her legs were stuck. Her nose burned. Panicked, she kicked with all her might, but it wasn't until she twisted her body that she was able to escape. She reached the surface, choking on lake water and gasping for air.

"See? It wasn't so bad."

Sarah remembered wanting to yank his rat-tail off his puny head. The experience had traumatized her, and she swore to never step foot inside another kayak again. The fear of tipping was too great.

"Wouldn't it be easier to pack the canoe?" she asked.

Scott stood up and handed her a paddle.

"We can't take the canoe where we're going." Scott winked.

The sky was sunless as they launched their boats into the lake, but the water was peaceful, which calmed Sarah's nerves. Apprehensive at first, she steered her kayak in a sporadic zig zag across the bay, but as she focused on using her core muscles to power her strokes, she began to paddle clean lines. Sarah loved the promise of excitement that a sunny day always brought, but she appreciated the cloudy day as a chance to rest her eyes. She watched the fish swim below through the window-clear lake. Scott was waiting patiently for her at the mouth of the bay.

"You're going to need this," he said, tossing a headlamp into her lap.

They paddled a little while longer before Scott took a sharp left turn into a tiny cove off the main water way. Sarah had paddled up and down the lake all her life and had never seen the entrance. The cove was well camouflaged by heavy overhanging branches. Sarah followed Scott to the shoreline. Once they beached their kayaks in the sand, Scott took Sarah's hand and led her to a dark opening in the mossy rockface.

"What is this place?" Sarah's voice echoed against the wet stone as they stepped inside. Instantly, the air temperature fluctuated from warm to cool. Their headlamps illuminated the walls, which glistened with mineral-rich water. It smelled damp and earthy.

"It's a cave system. Jeff and I discovered it when we were kids. We promised to keep it just between us ... until now."

"I can't believe you guys kept something like this from me!" Sarah looked around the inside of the narrow cave. Stalactites hung from the tall ceiling and Sarah could see a separate, smaller tunnel to the left. "What would Jeff say now that you've broken your promise?" Sarah teased.

"Oh, he knows we're here." Scott squeezed Sarah's hand. "I had to get his permission, of course."

Sarah smiled. She felt like the most special woman in the world.

"I want to show you something else." Scott led her through the cramped tunnel. They had to duck down quite a bit to make it through. The tunnel led to a larger cavern, which was also a dead end. Scott took her fingers and traced them along an imprint on the back wall. It looked like a clam shell with vertical striped lines across it.

"What is that?"

"It's a brachiopod fossil, entombed and preserved in the rock for millions of years."

Sarah was speechless. Her headlamp flashed against the cave wall revealing the shape of the brachiopod shell imbedded in the rock. She never imagined she'd find such beauty in a dark, dank place. The discovery was thrilling.

When they reached the mouth of the main cave, they were disappointed to see that it was raining. It poured so hard raindrops were bouncing off the lake.

"Damn, I packed a picnic and everything," Scott said overtop the noisy pitter patter of the downpour.

Sarah was determined to salvage the rest of their date. Feeling exhilarated from their adventure underground, she stripped off her t-shirt and shorts.

Scott's eyes grew wide before his face split into a grin. "What are you doing?" he yelled.

"Last one in is a rotten egg!" Sarah called. She raced across the small beach to the water's edge. Scott quickly caught up to her and wrapped his arms around her waist, lifting her feet off the ground. "Gotcha!"

"Put me down!" Sarah kicked her legs gleefully, but she was no match for his strength. Scott marched them deeper into the lake before tossing Sarah in and diving in right behind her. The water was warmer than the air. When they jumped up for air, they were standing face to face chest deep in the water. A romantic mist surrounded them. Scott's wise, green eyes reflected the ancient pines in the forest around them. Sarah found herself unable to look away. Scott leaned his head back to feel the rain on his face.

"I've never felt more alive! Sarah, I—"

"Scott, I need to talk to you," she blurted out. She couldn't wait any longer. She had to tell him.

Scott inched closer. She watched as his gaze flickered from her eyes down to her lips and back again. Scott slowly slipped his hands around Sarah's waist and pulled her to him. "Is this okay?" he asked.

Sarah nodded. It was better than okay. She gently

caressed the length of his back as Scott rubbed his thumbs up and down her waist with eagerness. Her heart bounced wildly around her chest as Scott slowly tilted his head and leaned forward. His lips had barely brushed against hers when suddenly they were interrupted by the roar of a motorboat ripping through the entrance of the cove at full speed. Scott and Sarah jumped apart as Jeff steered the boat toward them.

"What the hell are you doing?" Scott yelled over the noise of the motor.

"Sarah, I've got to get you back," said Jeff. "It's an emergency."

Sarah's body went cold with dread. "Did something happen to my mom? Is Mabel, okay?"

"They're both fine. Now hurry, get in the boat."

Fear stabbed Sarah's heart. "I'm not going anywhere until you tell me what's going on," she said, crossing her arms.

"It's your dad, Sarah. He's had a heart attack."

Chapter Sixteen

Sarah sat beside Mabel on the couch, clenching her sister's hand, as they awaited news of their father's prognosis. All the anger and hurt their fight had caused Sarah earlier had been washed away the moment she'd heard her father had suffered a heart attack. Scott and Jeff had offered to stay with them, but Sarah insisted she would call them as soon as she heard any news.

"Let me be here for you," Scott had pleaded with her.

Sarah felt extremely guilty for galivanting around the lake with Scott. Her father had been chopping wood when he'd keeled over, having suffered a heart attack. With everyone gathered around her, Sarah felt like she was suffocating. "Go home, Scott."

Scott shifted from one foot to another. His brow creased with uncertainty. There was a restlessness about him. "If you need anything, I'm right next door." He kissed the crown of her head before leaving.

Mabel squeezed Sarah's hand and offered her a weak smile. "Daddy will be okay," she told Sarah.

Their mother paced the kitchen floor. She had been on hold with the hospital in B.C for what seemed to be an eternity. When Mom suddenly stopped pacing, the tiny hairs on the back of Sarah's neck stood on end. Mom gasped and brought a hand to her mouth. She nodded a few times before whispering a weak "thank you" to the doctor. As she hung up the phone, Sarah knew. Her mother walked into the living room wearing the same pained expression that she had when grandma had died.

"They said it happened quickly. He didn't feel any pain."

Sarah ran to her mother and collapsed into her arms while Mabel groaned on the couch in agony. Regret kicked Sarah in the gut. Her last conversation with her father played on a loop in her head.

I'll never forgive you. I'll never forgive you. I'll never forgive you.

Terrible anguish struck Sarah's heart as she knew she would never have the chance to forgive her father.

"He told me he loved me," Sarah cried into her mother's shoulder, "and I didn't say it back to him." Sarah was devastated.

"Shh," her mother hushed. "Daddy knew." Mom collected Mabel into their fold and held her daughters tight. She had a stoic expression on her face, but Sarah knew her mother was struggling to remain strong. She knew Mom was holding it together for their sake.

The next day, they spent hours on the phone with a funeral home in B.C., making arrangements. Sarah was familiar with the fact that after someone you love died, there was an order of business that must be taken care of, even if all you wanted to do was crawl into bed with a box of tissues. Once the logistics were organized, Mom telephoned the airlines and booked three tickets to Vancouver.

"From Vancouver, we'll rent a car and drive to a motel just outside of Daddy's hometown," said Mom.

"Wouldn't it be easier to fly his body home to Ontario?" Sarah asked.

Mom shook her head. "His entire extended family lives in B.C. I know he would've wanted it this way. We'll bring his ashes home with us."

Over the next couple of days, the cottage phone rang off the hook as news of her father's death spread like wildfire. From the comfort of the couch, Sarah watched her mother work the phone like a busy switchboard operator from the 1950s. Mom put the calls on speaker phone so she could jot down notes or add items to the growing to-do list. The calls mostly consisted of questions or instructions from the funeral director and friends offering their condolences. Sarah was completely caught off guard when Emilee's French accent came through the line.

"Allo, Alice?"

"Yes, speaking." Mom's voice was strained. She pulled at the collar of her t-shirt as though it were strangling her.

"This is Emilee."

"Emilee. Yes. Hi." Mom cleared her throat.

Sarah moved from the couch to the kitchen and pulled up a seat next to her mother. "Hang up the phone," she whispered in her mother's ear. Her mother shooed her away like a pesky mosquito, but Sarah didn't budge.

"I've been in direct contact with the funeral home, and I was told the service is going to be held at a Catholic church?" Emilee asked.

"Yes. At St. Bridget's."

"You do know Jack was an atheist, right?"

"No, he was agnostic."

"Well, I should know. I was his paramour."

"How dare you. I am his wife!"

"What I meant to say is, I just don't think he would've wanted a—"

"How could you possibly know what he wanted? You knew each other for less than six months!" Mom aggressively organized the scattered papers on the kitchen table into neat piles. "I was married to Jack for almost twenty years."

There was silence on the other end of the line.

"I don't have time for this," Mom said. "If there's nothing else, I have a lot to prepare."

"Actually, there is."

"Yes?" Mom tapped her foot impatiently.

"I saw a copy of Jack's obituary, and I wasn't mentioned in it."

"Why would you be?"

"We were in love, Alice."

Mom stood up so quickly she almost knocked her chair backward. She paced the kitchen floor with her hands in fists. It looked like she wanted to pound something.

"I'll consider your request. Anything else?" Mom's voice was weak and faltering.

"Yes. One more thing. The funeral director told me that you were planning to have the reception catered in the basement of the church. I would love to host the reception in our home. We have a beautiful garden with a view of the ocean. I've already spoken to Jack's family, and they all think it's a lovely idea. I—"

"I'll think about it and get back to you." Mom hung up the phone and sat back down at the kitchen table, wringing her hands together.

"Are you okay?" Sarah asked. She rubbed her mother's back to calm her fidgeting. "What are you going to do?"

Mom took a deep breath. "I'll let her hold the reception at the home she shared with Daddy."

"What? No way. That's totally inappropriate."

"They were in love, Sarah. They were building a life together."

When tears spilled down her mother's soft cheeks, Sarah felt helpless. Her mother was suffering the loss of her father, for the second time in a matter of weeks, and Sarah worried her mother couldn't handle any more grief.

"Daddy loved you, too," she whispered in her mother's ear.

"I know, honey." Mom patted Sarah's hands and gave her a weak smile.

Sarah didn't want to leave her mother's side. She wanted to stay and help her organize the details for her father's funeral, but she had to go into town with Mabel. They needed dresses for the funeral.

Armed with their mother's Visa card, the girls drove into town on a mission. Thorny Bush had a heritage main street lined with old stone buildings that had been transformed into small shops, specialty stores, and restaurants. The town was originally a military settlement from the 1800s.

When they were younger, their grandmother would take them into town once or twice a summer for some shopping and lunch. Sarah recalled the first time she'd understood the heritage of the little town.

"This building used to house a jail," their grandmother had said as she stopped the girls outside a large square building constructed of sandstone. It had a unique clock tower on top.

"What is it used for today?" Sarah asked.

"It's the town hall." Her grandmother pointed to another building across the street. "What do you imagine the library used to be?"

Sarah couldn't imagine the building being anything else but a library. She knew it well. She carried two library cards in her purse, one for the city and one for the cottage. Every summer, Sarah would visit the Thorny Bush library and explore every shelf in the children's corner, always leaving with a stack of books so high she needed to use her chin to help balance the load to the car.

"Was it the General Store?" Sarah asked.

Grandma shook her head and pointed at the red brick tower with a gable roof on one side of the building. "It used to be the old fire hall. They built that tower so fire hoses could be hung to dry."

After shopping, their grandma would take them

for lunch at a popular restaurant in town that had a beautiful terrace overlooking the Long River. The waterway ran straight through the core of Thorny Bush in a canal. The River Café was known for its soups, sandwiches, coffee, and dessert.

Sarah now longed to have one last lunch with her grandmother on the terrace. She imagined pouring her heart out and having her grandmother listen and say all the right things that would make her feel better. Sarah worried she was forgetting the sound of her grandmother's voice. Sometimes, when Sarah missed her most, she would call her grandma's old number to hear her sweet voice on the answering machine. Mom didn't have the heart to disconnect Grandma's account yet.

"Maybe we could go to the River Café for lunch," Sarah said to Mabel.

Mabel ignored her invitation. She opened the door to the only clothing boutique in town. "Let's just get this over with," Mabel mumbled.

Miss Posy's Closet was located in a sandstone and yellow brick building that was originally a saddle and harness shop. Now, the store was lined with dresses, silk scarves, and leather handbags. Mabel grabbed a plain black fit-and-flare dress off the rack. "This will do."

Sarah was jealous of Mabel's straight figure. Clothes were made to fit her. She didn't even have to try the dress on. Meanwhile, Sarah was becoming claustrophobic in the boutique's tiny fitting room as she tried on dress after dress. The shop didn't have air conditioning, and Sarah was starting to sweat. The fitting room was so small her elbows hit the walls as she lifted yet another dress over her head and added it to the "no" pile. Too much cleavage.

"Try this one on," Mabel said, hanging a dark blue dress over the door.

The V-neck midi lace dress that Mabel picked was a perfect fit. The style reminded Sarah of a dress she had worn to her high school's semi-formal one year. Her dad had looked so proud when she and Julie emerged from her bedroom, all dressed up and ready for the dance.

"My little girl is all grown up," he had said with tears in his eyes. He had insisted on taking several photos before he dropped them off at the entrance of their high school gymnasium.

Mabel paid for the dresses, and they each left with a brown paper bag. Inside, their funeral dresses were wrapped in hot pink tissue paper. As they stepped out the door, they almost collided with Jeff and Scott's mom.

"Girls!" Mrs. Roberts quickly wrapped her arms around them. "I'm terribly sorry for your loss. My heart breaks for you."

Sarah's lips quivered. She blinked, willing herself not to cry in public. "Thank you."

Mrs. Roberts pulled away and placed a hand on her heart. "How's your mother coping?"

"As well as can be expected," said Mabel, checking her watch.

"Scott and Jeff told me your family asked for space, but I'm right next door if you need anything. I've organized a meal train and I—"

"That's very kind of you," Mabel interrupted. She looped her arm through Sarah's arm and gently guided her toward the car. "Thank you, Mrs. Roberts. We have to get back—"

"Sarah! Before you go, just one more thing!" called Mrs. Roberts.

Sarah paused mid-step and turned to face Mrs. Roberts again. Sarah wanted nothing more than to escape the look of pity on her face, but Sarah would never be rude to someone so well-intentioned as Mrs. Roberts.

"Yes?"

"Scott has been worried sick about you. He's not been himself. If he calls again, perhaps you could talk to him for a minute? Just to let him know how you're doing. It might help you to talk about what you're going through." Mrs. Roberts' eyes glistened with a sympathetic sorrow.

Sarah wondered if from now on, people would always look at her the way Mrs. Roberts was looking at her now. She couldn't stand it for another minute. She nodded her head. "Yes, Mrs. Roberts."

The moment they got back to the cottage, Sarah went to her bedroom to hang up her new dress.

"What the fuck is this?" Sarah heard Mabel say from the kitchen. Sarah went to investigate. Mabel thrusted a copy of their father's obituary into her hands.

Jack Williams is survived by his loving wife, Alice, and their two daughters, Mabel and Sarah, and his partner, Emilee Vaillancourt.

"How could you?" Mabel glared at their mother, who sat at the kitchen table, massaging her temples.

"It's what Daddy would have wanted, Mabel. As much as I want to, I can't erase her from his life. It's the right thing to do."

"What about the reception?" Sarah asked. "We're still having it in the church basement, right?"

"Daddy's Uncle John thinks I've got enough on my plate. He's persuaded me to hand the reins over to Emilee. Apparently, the home they shared has a beautiful garden for the reception. Much nicer than a musty old basement."

"I'm not setting foot in her house!" Mabel stomped off to her bedroom.

Sarah didn't like the idea either, but she knew it must have been a heartbreaking decision for her mother to make. She wished Mabel would put herself in their mother's shoes for once.

"I'll go finish packing," Sarah said, not knowing what else to do or say.

Her mother looked up from the mountain of paperwork before her. "Don't forget to pack a raincoat. B.C. is damp."

Sarah piled her clothes in neat squares on her bed before placing them into her tweed and leather rolling suitcase. She added a sweater in case it was cold and a rain jacket. Sarah thought it was odd that a place called the Sunshine Coast would have rainy weather.

The last time Sarah had traveled to B.C., she was a toddler. Her family had gone to visit her grandfather, Gilbert, who lived in a tiny cottage in a beach community called Hubert's Creek. His wife, Sarah's grandmother, had died before Sarah was born. Gilbert was a talented writer. When he was younger, he was a journalist for national newspapers and magazines, but after he retired, he published a book of poems about nature and conservation topics. Sarah liked to think she'd inherited his writing gene. Sarah couldn't remember Gilbert or her first trip out to B.C. because she was too young. All her memories came from old photographs or from stories her parents told her.

"You said your first swear word on that trip," her father had said one lazy Saturday afternoon as they flipped through photo albums together on the couch. As a child, Sarah couldn't fathom that she had done such a thing. She was curious. "What word did I say, Daddy?"

"Well, your grandfather was an impatient driver, and he swore like a sailor as he drove us up and down the coast in his pickup truck. Our vacation was coming to an end, and he was driving us back to the airport in Vancouver. We were parked on the ferry, and you climbed into his lap and started to pretend you were driving. You honked the horn and yelled 'Jesus Christ' out the window."

While Sarah couldn't remember the time she had spent with her grandfather, she did remember the feeling. If she closed her eyes, she could still taste the salt on the breeze. She could feel the warmth of a wrinkled hand clasped around her little, dimpled one, guiding her down a long, sandy beach. Sadly, Gilbert died not long after their trip out west. Sarah had wished her whole life that he had lived longer, then she would have flown out to B.C. every summer to visit with her grandfather. He had built boats as a hobby, and he would have taught her how to fish. She liked to think they would have written stories together, too. She pictured him writing the beginning of a story before licking a stamp and sending it to Sarah in the mail. She would have written the ending and mailed it back. She had dreamed of traveling to B.C. again, but she'd never imagined it would be for her father's funeral.

"Sarah, honey?" Her mother knocked gently on her door. "Scott's here to see you."

"I'll be out in a minute!" Sarah got off the bed and caught a glimpse of herself in the mirror. Normally, she would have applied a coat of lip gloss and run a brush through her hair, but it didn't matter anymore.

"He's waiting for you on the deck," her mother said when she emerged from her room.

Sarah found Scott sitting on their picnic table. He looked effortlessly handsome in a pair of navy-blue board shorts and a clean white t-shirt. His messy curls were naturally highlighted from spending so much time in the sun. Scott jumped up to greet her.

"Want to take a walk?" he asked.

Sarah nodded. "Okay."

They slowly wandered side by side through the

pine grove in silence. The path was narrow, and electricity ran up Sarah's arm each time Scott's arm grazed hers. The sunlight filtered through the canopy, highlighting the colors of summer—vibrant green leaves, mauve wildflowers, and bright blue skies. Sarah held out her hand and gently caressed tree bark as she passed by. The murmur of the water was comforting.

"I tried calling you a couple of times," he said, breaking the silence. "How are you holding up?"

His genuine kindness made tears spring to her eyes. "I'm fine. Thanks."

Scott's eyebrows knitted together. "You don't look fine. I wish you'd talk to me."

Sarah stopped walking and crossed her arms. "I don't understand why, when I'm the one supposed to be grieving, I'm also responsible for supporting everyone else and their feelings. It's exhausting! There. Is that what you wanted to hear, Scott?"

"I just want to be here for you. That's all." Scott reached out to touch her elbow, but Sarah pulled away.

"I don't need you to save me, Scott."

"That's not what I'm trying to do. Listen, I know you felt something that day on the lake. I felt it, too. I—"

"That day on the lake was a mistake."

A pained expression came over Scott's face. He shook his head. "You don't mean that."

Sarah wanted nothing more than to collapse into his arms and let him take care of her, but she knew she was no longer the same person that Scott had been falling for. Her father's death had changed her, and she didn't know if Scott could love this new, messier version of herself. If he couldn't, Sarah knew herself well enough to know she wouldn't handle it well. It would break her. Sarah needed to protect herself before things went any further. "You're an incredible person, Scott, but it would never work. When summer is over, we're going our separate ways. You're going back to Kingston, and I'm moving to Montreal."

"Sarah, at least let me be here for you. I want to help. I—"

"You can help by giving me some space!" Frustrated by his persistence, Sarah whipped around and started the short hike back to her cottage.

The pine grove, which had once been a special sanctuary that bonded them together, was now a wall that would keep them separated.

Chapter Seventeen

"You didn't have to do this," Mom said as Jeff pulled their car up to the departure drop-off area at the Ottawa airport. "Thank you, sweetheart."

"I wanted to," he said, smiling at her. "Now you don't have to worry about paying for long-term parking. It's the least I could do."

"Give Pete lots of extra cuddles for me," said Mom as she opened the passenger side door and stepped out of the car.

"Don't worry, Mrs. Williams, he's going to train with me. He'll get plenty of exercise." Jeff drummed his fingers against the steering wheel. His eye's met Sarah's in the rear-view mirror. "Car sick?"

Sarah shook her head. "I'm nervous about the flight."

"Oh, yeah?" He turned in his seat to face her. "Do you want to know what you have to do in the event of an emergency?"

Sarah's eyes widened as she realized she didn't know what she was supposed to do if the plane went down.

"If the plane is going to crash, just put your head between your knees…"

Sarah listened intently. "Uh huh."

"And kiss your ass goodbye!"

Sarah smacked him on the shoulder as he chuckled at his own joke.

"Not funny!" But Sarah couldn't help but smile. Jeff had a way of lifting even her sourest of moods.

After grabbing their luggage from the trunk, they waved to Jeff from the curb. He'd be back in a week to pick them up.

The airport was busy with passenger traffic. People were coming and going from all over the world. They stood in the middle of the lobby, watching the scene unfold. The building itself was a large steel rectangle that supported floor to ceiling windows. The sunrise was almost blinding. With their passports in hand, they got their tickets, checked their luggage, and went through security. Once they reached their gate, her mother placed a tiny pink pill in Sarah's hand.

"It's Gravol, honey," she whispered. "Take it now, and it will settle your stomach for the flight."

Sarah gave her mother a grateful smile. She placed the anti-nausea medication under her tongue. It tasted like chalk.

"I call the aisle seat," Mabel said once it was time to board their flight. Nobody argued. They all knew Mabel had the bladder of a five-year-old and would have to go every hour on the flight.

"Take the window seat," their mother offered Sarah. "I'll sit in the middle."

Despite being nervous about the flight, Sarah found liftoff exhilarating. She squeezed her mother's hand as she watched Ottawa shrink to the size of ants. Sarah was amazed at how straight and orderly the roads and neighbourhoods looked from a bird's-eye view. As soon as the seatbelt light turned off, Mabel unbuckled her belt and left to use the washroom.

"The last time we made this trip together, you were only two years old," her mother said. "You were an angel on that flight. While other infants cried bloody murder throughout the four-hour trip, you sat happily beside me, eating your snacks. I remember cutting out paper dolls for you to play with."

Sarah snuggled up against her mother's shoulder.

She felt comforted to be close to her mother. She yawned, feeling the Gravol kick in. The side effect of the medication was that it made her sleepy. Her mother patted her cheek. "Rest now. When you wake up, we'll be by the ocean."

Sarah snoozed for about twenty minutes before she woke up with a kink in her neck. She spent the rest of the flight trying to get comfortable. She tried to distract herself from the pain by eating airplane food and watching *Sliding Doors* starring Gwyneth Paltrow. Sarah was fascinated by the film because it alternated between two storylines, showing the two different paths the main character's life would take depending on whether she caught a train or not. Sarah knew all too well how a split second could send your life in a completely different direction.

After their plane touched down in Vancouver, the women collected their luggage, rented a car, and began the two-hour trip to Hubert's Creek. On the scenic route, the surrounding nature called out to Sarah. She didn't know if it was the fresh smell of the rain or the soft whisper on the lull of the breeze, but she felt like the North Shore Mountains were welcoming her back. Even though she had only spent a short period of time in mountains on a family vacation sixteen years ago, it felt like she belonged here. She understood her father's incessant pull to British Columbia. She felt closer to him than ever.

"This is it," her mother said, pulling into the Sand and Sea Motel.

Hubert's Creek possessed a stunning blend of beaches and forest. The main strip in town was lined with pottery shops, paint studios, and art galleries. The residents had painted a mandala at the base of the pier. It was a true arts and culture scene.

"It looks exactly the same as it did the last time we stayed here," her mother said as they walked into their medium-sized unit.

There were two queen-size beds covered in shiny green comforters. The room also had a dark blue pull-out couch, a mahogany desk, and black office chair. Sarah's mom inspected the room for cleanliness. Once she was satisfied, she placed her suitcase on the luggage rack and began to unpack. "Don't go barefoot on the carpet," she reminded the girls. "You could get a fungus."

"Complimentary continental breakfast is included," Mabel said, reading from a brochure off the desk.

"Anyone want to go for a walk?" said Sarah. "I need to stretch my legs."

"I need a nap," Mabel said, crawling into one of the beds fully clothed.

"I wish I could, honey," said her mother. She took a black dress out of her suitcase and hung it in the closet. "I have too much to do for tomorrow. I'm meeting with the funeral home director in an hour to go over the final details. You go on ahead, though."

The beach was a two-minute walk from their motel. The overcast skies were beginning to part ways, inviting the sunshine through. Sarah was glad she wore her running shoes since the beach was rocky, spanning miles of the coastline. Seagulls squawked their cacophonous call as they soared overhead. Large pieces of driftwood decorated the beach like works of art. Sarah stopped to pick up a lone piece of sea glass. She tucked the blue frosted beach jewel into her pocket. It was washed smooth from years of tumbling through saltwater waves. A gift from nature.

A young family passed by with two little girls in gumboots carrying pails and shovels. Sarah smiled as she recalled a story her dad had told her about her first time harvesting mussels in B.C.

"We collected so many we had a mussels feast," her dad had said. "We gathered around Grandpa's table and shared a bottle of wine as we talked about our adventure that day. Meanwhile, you sat quietly in your highchair, happily eating your supper. That's when we noticed you had eaten an entire bucket of mussels all to yourself! At two years old! Grandpa was so proud."

Sarah decided she would order steamed mussels in a white wine broth for dinner that night. For old time's sake. The beach appeared to be a prime location to launch kayaks. As she watched a small group of friends paddle their kayaks out to sea, Sarah couldn't help but think of Scott. In that moment, she realized how much she missed him. She regretted asking him for space. She worried she had ruined everything and wondered if he would be there for her when she got back.

What if he's already decided to move on? she thought.

She wished she could just pick up the phone and call him, but she didn't have any privacy in their motel room. She'd call him on her cellphone, but she had run out of minutes. Sarah couldn't afford to buy more. She needed to save every penny for university. Sarah decided she would have to wait until she got back to the cottage to explain.

Early the next morning, their motel phone rang.

"Hello?" Sarah answered. Her voice was groggy from sleep.

"Good morning!" greeted the lady at the front desk. "This is your wake-up call."

Sarah turned over and gently shook her mother awake. "It's time to get up."

"Why so early?" Mabel moaned from the

neighboring bed. "The funeral isn't until 11:00."

Mom sat up in bed and rubbed her face. "I want to get there early. I need to make sure everything is just right."

After they showered and dressed in their funeral attire, Mom insisted they grab a muffin from the complimentary breakfast counter.

"You need to eat something," she pleaded. "You'll need your strength today."

Sarah took the teensiest bite to appease her mother, but she could barely swallow. She was too upset to eat. She wasn't ready to say goodbye to her father.

It was a good thing Mom had decided to leave early because she took a wrong turn somewhere along the way, and when they finally arrived at the church, they only had 15 minutes to spare.

"Are you sure this is the right place?" Mabel asked, looking around. The parking lot was deserted.

"Yes, Mabel."

Their mother looked annoyed as she straightened out her skirt and hurried up the church steps. Sarah and Mabel followed closely behind.

Inside, the church was empty. Their high heels clicked against the marble floor as they searched for the priest.

"May I help you?"

They turned to see a cheerful woman with round cheeks and a rusty perm, standing with a clipboard. She held out her hand. "My name is Susan. I am a volunteer here at St. Bridget's."

"Hi, yes, we're here for Jack Williams' funeral," said Mom shaking her hand. "We're his family."

"I'm so sorry for your loss," said Susan placing a hand over her heart, "but, I'm afraid you have the wrong church, dear. Jack Williams' funeral isn't being held here. I believe his wife moved the service to Blessed Sacrament."

"I'm his wife!" Mom blurted. Without missing a beat, she marched straight past Susan and out the front doors of the church.

"I'm sorry," Sarah mouthed to Susan before she and Mabel ran to keep up with their mother.

After whipping into a gas station to get directions, they learned Blessed Sacrament Parish was only a five-minute drive down the road. They would make it just in time. When they pulled up to Blessed Sacrament, they saw Great Uncle John standing outside the front doors with a woman who Sarah recognized to be Emilee from her father's photograph. They greeted guests as they arrived at the service. With her head held high, Sarah's mother walked right past them through the open doors of the church and found a seat in the front row, which was reserved for family. Mabel stuck her nose up at Emilee and followed suit. Sarah, however, couldn't let Emilee get away with this. Rage consumed her. She was quivering with anger, and her nostrils flared as she spoke. "Nobody told us that you changed the church."

Emilee's eyes widened before she looked to Great Uncle John, who shrugged his shoulders.

"Mon cheri, I'm so sorry," Emilee said. "I don't know how this happened, I—"

"We're his fucking family!" Sarah screamed.

Sarah didn't care if the entire church had heard her. She had never felt more disrespected in her life. She marched into the church but couldn't get past the entranceway. Everyone was looking. Panic overcame her. She was breathing heavily, and her vision blurred. She wasn't ready to bury her dad. An anxiety attack was about to put a strangle hold over her when, suddenly, someone in the church caught her attention. Sarah blinked. She couldn't believe her eyes. Standing in the back row of the parish, looking handsome and stoic in a dark blue suit, was Scott. Their eyes locked, only for a moment, but it gave Sarah all the strength she needed to join her mother and sister at her father's funeral.

The service was a meaningful celebration of her father's life. Her mother had ordered wildflower arrangements of daisies, black-eyed Susans, and bluebells to surround her father's carved wooden urn. They were the same flowers that lined the road to the cottage. Sarah was comforted as she listened to the priest speak about the fleeting nature of life and the symbolism behind cherry blossoms. Like her father's life, the life of a cherry blossom is short, too.

When the service was over, the guitarist sang *Pussy Willows, Cattails,* a song by Gordon Lightfoot, as the guests followed his urn out of the church. Gordon Lightfoot was her father's favorite artist.

Outside, Sarah searched the busy parking lot for Scott, but her mother rushed her into the car.

"We were practically late for the funeral, Sarah. I don't want to miss your father's reception."

Begrudgingly, Sarah got into the car and buckled up her seatbelt. "How did that happen?"

"The Funeral Director was extremely apologetic," said Mom. "Apparently, Emilee had made the request to switch the church with the funeral home's receptionist, who mistook her for his wife. It seems there was a miscommunication between Emilee and the rest of the family, and somewhere along the way, they forgot to tell us."

"Regardless, the service was beautiful, Mom," said Mabel from the back seat. "Daddy would have loved it." She leaned forward and squeezed their mother's shoulder. Sarah nodded and squeezed her mother's hand that rested on the gear shift.

The home their father shared with Emilee was right on the ocean, a modern custom-designed cedar home built in harmony with its natural surroundings. They walked through a white gate at the side of the house and into their father's flourishing garden. Someone had laid a bouquet of flowers beneath the cherry tree. Sarah stood at the makeshift memorial for a moment with her mother and sister. Looking out over the ocean, Sarah knew why her father had wanted to live here. The lure was Mother Nature herself.

"Alice!"

Sarah cringed when she heard the French accent.

"Here she comes," Mabel whispered through her teeth.

Mom put on a brave face and turned to greet her husband's lover. She was caught by surprise when Emilee grabbed her by the shoulders and kissed each cheek.

"You must forgive me for the miscommunication," Emilee said. "I thought Johnny was going to tell you, and he thought I was going to tell you." Emilee grabbed two glasses of white wine from a caterer who stood nearby with a silver tray. She handed Alice a glass. "Jack's service was beautiful. You did a wonderful job, Alice."

Mom took a sip of wine and smiled. "You have a beautiful home, Emilee. The memorial beneath the cherry tree is a nice touch, too. Thank you for hosting."

Sarah was shocked by her mother's sincerity and grace. Her mother wasn't trying to pretend to like Emilee, but it was as if she was genuinely trying to connect with her.

"You'll have to excuse me. I must go greet the guests that just arrived. Please get something to eat. I'll be right back," said Emilee.

"I want to slap that stupid smile off her face," Mabel said as Emilee hustled toward the gate.

"Mabel, please keep your voice down," said Mom. She took a gulp of wine.

"Why are you being so nice to her? She stole your husband!" said Mabel.

"Because I don't want your father's reception turned into an episode of *The Jerry Springer Show*," Mom whispered through her teeth.

"So you let Emilee treat you like a doormat?" Sarah asked.

"Girls, this doesn't have to be a big dramatic showdown. I'm not in any way excusing their behavior, but I am in the process of forgiving them. It may be hard for you to understand, but I've accepted that my marriage ended the way it did for a reason."

"Yeah, and her name is Emilee," Mabel muttered under her breath.

Mom looked out to sea. Beyond the garden, the water rushed up the shoreline, breaking on the rocks. "Oddly enough, coming to their home has brought me comfort. I don't know if you noticed, but Emilee talks with her hands a lot, and I saw that she was wearing your father's watch. It made me realize that she really did love your dad, and I take comfort in knowing he was surrounded by love when he died."

Sarah was in awe of her mother's strength. "After all that's happened, I don't know how you do it."

"A lot has happened over the past year, and I've learned that I'm the one who has the power to let go of the pain."

When Emilee returned to take Mom for a tour of the house, Sarah and Mabel bowed out and made their way to a caterer holding a tray of smoked salmon and cream cheese hors d'oeuvres. Sarah was famished. She hadn't eaten all day. She had just stuffed one into her mouth whole when she felt a tap on her shoulder.

"Sarah, Mabel. Hi."

"Scott!" Sarah said with her mouth full. She quickly covered her mouth with her hand and swallowed as fast as she could.

"Scott! Thank you for coming," said Mabel, resting her hors d'oeuvre on a tiny white napkin.

"I can't believe you came," Sarah said.

"I wanted to be here for you," he said, looking directly at Sarah.

"I wanted to call you. I—"

"Sarah!" Her Great Uncle John popped out of nowhere and linked his arm through hers. "I'm sorry to interrupt, but I want to introduce you to your second cousin, Meghan, before she leaves."

Before Sarah could protest, he patted her hand and pulled her along.

"She writes for a parenting magazine in Vancouver."

Sarah tried to concentrate as Meghan hummed and hawed over the politics of the publishing world. Sarah nodded politely, but she could only focus on Scott and Mabel. She wondered what they were talking about.

"Sarah, are you feeling okay?" Meghan asked.

Sarah shook her head. "I'm sorry. It's been a tough day..." Sarah trailed off, watching Scott and Mabel embrace.

"Of course," said Meghan, rummaging through her purse. She pulled out a cream business card. "If you ever have any questions, don't hesitate to call me." She slipped the rectangular card into Sarah's hand and gave her a hug. "I'm so sorry for your loss. It was lovely to meet you."

Sarah twirled the card in her hands as she searched the grounds for Scott. She found Mabel standing alone by the cherry tree.

"Scott said to give you his best," Mabel said as Sarah approached.

"He left?"

"He had to catch his flight."

"So soon?" Sarah was incredibly disappointed.

"He couldn't afford to take any more time off work."

Sarah felt guilty. "He must have spent a good chunk of his savings for school on his ticket."

Mabel nodded.

"What did you guys talk about?" Sarah was attempting to act nonchalant about it, but Mabel could see right through her.

"God, you're nosy."

"Girls!" interrupted their mother, waving them over to a low point on the property. "It's time to scatter Daddy's ashes."

The plan was to scatter some of his ashes in the ocean and bury his urn in the cemetery near the cottage. Sarah wished Scott had been able to stay and hold her hand through this. She took off her heels and reluctantly followed the family through a gate at the back of the property. From the beach, the entranceway was almost hidden by bushes. With everyone gathered at the water's edge, Sarah and Mabel dug a trench in the shape of a heart, and their mother filled it with some of their father's cremated remains. Sarah wept as the tide came in and swept her father's ashes out to sea.

Chapter Eighteen

Sarah wished their trip to B.C. wouldn't end. When she walked along the beach, she could feel her dad was close. She worried she would lose that feeling once they left.

"Can we stay a few extra days?" Sarah begged. "Please?"

Her mother carefully wrapped her father's urn in a sweater and packed it into her carry-on suitcase.

"Sarah, I have a lot to take care of back at home before we bury your father. Pete is waiting for us, too."

"I'm sure Jeff wouldn't mind taking care of him for a couple more days."

"Sarah, you and Mabel have to go back to work. Fall is around the corner, and we need to get you ready for school. I'm sorry."

"We didn't even get to see Grandpa's boat."

Grandpa had been a writer by trade, but was also a passionate boat builder. At the funeral, Sarah had learned through her Great Uncle John that Grandpa's handmade double-ended highliner was on display in the Sunshine Coast Museum.

"You can come back next year. Uncle John has even offered you a place to stay if you want to work out here next summer."

It was a generous offer, but Sarah couldn't imagine spending her summers anywhere but at the cottage. She reluctantly joined her mother in packing.

Their four-hour flight home was uneventful. After their plane touched down, they found Jeff outside the arrivals gate, waiting to collect them in her mother's silver Taurus. Pete sat in the passenger seat, panting. He stuck his head out the window when he saw them.

"Boy, did we miss you," said Jeff.

Sarah smiled. She was grateful for the warm welcome home. She had missed him, too. Jeff hopped out of the driver's seat and helped the women with their luggage. Before driving them back to the cottage, Jeff handed her mother a pile of envelopes.

"I stopped by your house and picked up the mail for you."

"Thank you, Jeff," her mother said. She placed the mail in her oversize purse. "I don't know what we would've done without you."

When they were back at the cottage, settling in, Sarah sat on her mother's bed petting Pete. She was procrastinating unpacking her suitcase. She watched as Mom rifled through the mail.

"Sarah!" Mom gasped. There was a sense of urgency in her voice.

Sarah stopped patting Pete. "What's the matter?"

"There's a letter here for you." She handed Sarah a crisp white envelope. "It's from Dad. He must have sent it before he died."

Mabel appeared in the doorframe. Mom handed Sarah a letter opener that her father had whittled himself. He had given it to Mom on their fifth wedding anniversary. Sarah sliced the envelope open. She gently pulled out a thin piece of paper and unfolded it. Her eyes blurred with tears. She couldn't read it. Mabel joined Sarah on the bed and wrapped her arm around her shoulders. Mabel gently took the letter from Sarah's trembling hands and cleared her throat. Her voice shook as she read:

"Dear Sarah,

I have made some big mistakes, but marrying your mother and having you was not one of them. I wish I had handled this situation differently. I know I am guilty of splitting the family apart, but I believe it is for the better. I never intended to hurt you or cause you pain. I love and respect you for who you are and how you are handling this.

    Love,
    Dad"

Tears dripped down Mabel's cheeks and splashed onto the letter, making watermarks. Sarah gently took the letter from Mabel's hands and read it again to herself. It was short and to the point. Sarah felt he was sorry. She held the letter to her heart, grateful for the gift of his last loving words.

"He must have written it after you called him," her mother said. She placed her cool hand on Sarah's forearm and gave it a squeeze. "I told you he knew. Parents know these things." Her mother winked, causing Sarah to laugh through her tears. Her mother was always right.

"Why don't you two go relax in the lounge chairs on the deck while I make dinner? The sunshine will do you good."

The girls nodded in agreement and went outside to soak up some vitamin D. They pulled their lounge chairs into the sun and sat, silently watching the yellow rays hit the small waves on the lake below. A fish jumped out of the lake, probably to swallow a water bug, and birds flew over the pine trees in the distance. It felt good for the soul, being back at the cottage, amid its rugged natural beauty.

"It's nice to be back," said Sarah. She snuggled deeper into the lounge cushion.

Pine Lake was a cottage paradise. If she listened closely, Sarah could hear relaxed barbecue parties of friends and families happening all around the bay. It was a pleasant reminder of what life was all about, having fun with the ones you loved.

"Do you have feelings for Scott?" Mabel asked, interrupting Sarah's thoughts.

Sarah's mind scrambled. She wasn't prepared for Mabel's question and didn't want to cause any more hurt within the family. If she lied to Mabel, it could potentially open the door for her sister to go after Scott. If she told Mabel the truth, it could possibly clear the way for Sarah to pursue Scott. She decided to be totally honest with Mabel since it was her father's lies that had caused her family so much hurt.

"Mabel, I do have feelings for Scott. I have for a long time." Sarah paused. "I'm in love with him."

Mabel didn't respond. Her sudden silence made Sarah uncomfortable. She fidgeted in her chair. Sarah was beginning to regret telling her sister when Mabel finally spoke.

"He's in love with you, too."

Sarah's jaw dropped. "How do you know?"

"He told me. At Daddy's funeral."

Sarah sat straight up. "What did he say?"

"He was worried that you would be angry with him because you asked him for space. He decided to chance it and booked the flight, promising himself he would just stand in the background. He wanted to be there for you in case you needed him."

Sarah pulled her knees to her chest and bit her lip. The dam was about to burst. "But what if it doesn't work out? It could ruin everything, Mabel. I'm scared."

"Why wouldn't it work out?"

Sarah rested her chin on her knees and gazed out at the water, thinking. "We're both going away to different schools in separate cities."

"Montreal and Kingston aren't that far away."

"What if he breaks my heart? Or worse, I end up breaking his?"

"If Daddy's death has taught me anything, it's that life is too short to be afraid of the 'what ifs.' Scott loves you and treats you right. If you get a chance at love, take it."

"You still feel that way even after your breakup with Benny?"

Mabel shrugged. "I couldn't see it before, but I'm realizing now that I allowed Benny to be my priority while allowing myself to be his option."

"Oh, Mabel." Sarah reached across and squeezed Mabel's forearm. "One day someone will walk into your life, and you'll see why it didn't work out with Benny."

Mabel smiled. "I'm not afraid anymore to have lost what wasn't meant to be."

Sarah admired Mabel's courage. Her sister had fallen apart after Benny broke up with her, but she continued on despite being hurt. She was unstoppable.

Sarah lay back in her lounge chair and took in the beauty of her childhood paradise. Her gaze followed the golden bars of sunlight through the majestic pine trees. She thought about her conversation with Mabel, but unlike her sister, Sarah didn't know what her father's death was supposed to teach her. The answer came to her on the haunting echo of a loon call, reminding her that she had waited until it was too late to tell her father how much she had loved him. Sarah sat up with a jolt.

I'll tell Scott tonight.

When supper was ready, the women gathered around the picnic table. Their mother had made a delicious summer pasta with fresh tomatoes, garlic, and basil from a meal train basket that Mrs. Roberts had organized for their family. Sarah sprinkled parmesan cheese and pepper on top. It felt wonderful to share a comforting meal with two of the people she admired most in her life. Their strength and soft hearts had inspired her.

"The priest called while I was making dinner. Daddy's burial is scheduled for next Saturday," their mother said, pouring herself a glass of red wine.

"Let us know if you need any help with the preparations," said Mabel.

"Julie will want to come," said Sarah. "Is it okay if she stays with us for a few days afterwards?"

"Of course," Mom said. "We need all the love and support we can get right now." She took a sip of wine. "Girls, I have some other news."

Sarah slurped the end of a spaghetti strand through a tiny hole in her lips and placed her fork down. She wanted to give her mother her full attention. "Tell us," she said, patting her lips with a linen napkin.

"I've decided to go back to school."

"Really?" Mabel asked. "What are you going to study?"

"Art."

For as long as Sarah could remember, her mother had loved diving into creative projects. She always found and appreciated beauty in the world. It was evident in the way she arranged flowers for the dinner table or in the soft fabrics with unique prints she had bought to sew dresses for them when they were younger. She was even artistic in the way she made salad, decorating the dish with sliced radishes, spiralized beets, shaved carrots, and sprinkled microgreens.

"That's great, Mom!" said Sarah.

"When we were in Hubert's Creek, I went for a walk and wandered in and out of the galleries and art shops along the main strip. It felt like home, and I remembered why I loved art so much in the first place."

"Daddy would be proud," said Mabel.

"After all that has happened and with everyone moving on, I knew it was time to return to my craft."

Mabel raised her wine glass. "To new beginnings."

After the dinner dishes had been washed and put away, Sarah took Pete on his third walk of the evening. Each time she walked him, she would pass the Robert's cottage to see if Scott's truck was in the driveway. Still empty.

He must have been scheduled for the afternoon shift at the beach.

When Sarah reached the front door of their cottage, she heard Scott's pickup come up the steep gravel hill. She fought the urge to race over and jump into his arms. She anticipated they would share their first kiss and wanted to be prepared for the moment she had been dreaming of since she was twelve years old.

Sarah slipped into a green floral mini dress that was both sweet and sexy. The flowy dress had a deep V shape on the back that accentuated her toned muscles. The thought of Scott's hands touching her bare shoulder blades made her shiver. Sarah brushed her teeth, twice, and gargled with mouthwash. She collected her hair into a loose ponytail and added a peach blush to her cheeks. She decided against lip gloss. She did not want their first kiss to be a sticky mess.

When she was ready, Sarah slipped out the sliding glass door and headed over to the Roberts' cottage through the pine grove. The tall trees were slow dancing, solo, in the warm summer breeze. Their high branches occasionally brushed against one another's needles. The new growth on their tips looked like a wet paint brush dipped in light green paint. When Sarah was younger, she would harvest the tips with her grandmother to make tea.

"It's full of vitamin C," her grandma had said as she steeped the tips in a teapot.

The young tips yielded a light, almost lemony

flavour.

Sarah picked a light green tip and brought the pointy bristles to her nose. The sap-scented needles calmed her nerves. She jogged the rest of the way to the Roberts' front door and knocked impatiently. She could not wait to see Scott.

"To what do we owe the pleasure?" Jeff asked as he swung open the front door. Sweat dripped down his forehead. His gray t-shirt was soaked in sweat under his armpits.

"Hey!" Sarah said breathlessly. "Is Scott here?"

"I just got back from a run. Hold on." Jeff turned his head back. "Scott!"

Mrs. Roberts came to the door behind Jeff. "Sarah, sweetheart, it's so good to see you. How are you holding up?"

"Hi, Mrs. Roberts. We got the card and flowers you sent for my dad's funeral. We're so thankful for the kindness your family has shown us. I know my mother is so grateful for the meal train, too."

"Would you like to come in for tea?"

Sarah shifted her weight between her feet. She needed to talk to Scott. She couldn't wait any longer.

"Actually, I'm here to see Scott. Is he here?"

"Yes, he's down by the dock with—"

"Thanks, Mrs. Roberts," Sarah said taking a few steps backwards. "We'll have tea another time!" She waved goodbye before turning on her heel. She raced toward the stairs that led to the Roberts' dock.

"You're welcome anytime!" Mrs. Roberts called after her.

When Sarah reached the top of the stairs, she tightened her ponytail and tucked the lose hairs around her ears. She licked her nude lips and took a deep breath. This was the moment that was about to change everything. She hurried down the wooden stairs. She saw Scott standing at the end of the dock. He stood with his hands in his pockets, staring out at the horizon. The sun was setting, turning the sky the color of sweet summer strawberries. Sarah could not have imagined a more romantic setting for her first kiss with Scott. She tiptoed up behind him, eager to wrap her arms around his waist and bury her face in his broad back. Suddenly, a pair of manicured hands slipped through Scott's arms from the front and wrapped around his waist. Scott took his hands out of his pockets and held the woman in his arms. He gently rocked her back and forth.

"Scott?" Sarah's voice was barely audible. Her heart began to race.

Scott whipped his head around. There, in his arms, was Britney.

ALYSSA DELLE PALME

Chapter Nineteen

"He's a dick," said Julie, trying to console Sarah over the phone. "He doesn't deserve you."

"I thought he loved me. I'm an idiot for trusting him."

"No, you can't blame yourself for his actions."

Self-doubt consumed Sarah. She knew she had caught Scott off-guard when she surprised him at the dock.

"Sarah, hi." His eyes had widened. He looked like a child who had been caught stealing a chocolate bar from a convenience store.

Sarah had stared straight past him and locked eyes with Britney. She looked as if she had been crying. Britney snuggled deeper into Scott's shoulder, hiding her face. Sarah's lips trembled. "I'm sorry to interrupt," she said. She took off running for the stairs.

"Sarah, wait!" Scott had called after her, but Sarah refused to let them see her cry. She took the stairs two at a time.

Sarah squeezed her eyes shut. She could not get the image of Britney in Scott's arms out of her head.

"When are you leaving?" Sarah asked Julie. She needed her best friend now more than ever.

"First thing tomorrow morning. I'll be there nice and early to help with the setup for your dad's burial."

"L-Y-L-A-S," said Sarah.

"Love you like a sister."

Sarah hung up the phone. It was their tradition since grade seven to end their conversations using the acronym. They had read it in a novel once and used it ever since. They closed their letters the same way.

Sarah sat down in a kitchen chair and laced up her running shoes. For her father's memorial, she was responsible for making mementos for the service, and she needed to collect natural materials.

"What if we invited our friends and family to write memories of Daddy on pieces of paper they can hang onto a memorial tree with brown twine?" Sarah had asked her mother. "Or maybe instead of paper, I could gather fallen birch bark and cut it up into smaller pieces of paper?"

"That's a lovely idea," her mother had said.

Sarah stepped outside. The sweet, refreshing scent of pine filled her nostrils. She picked up her pace and galloped past the Roberts' cottage like a horse wearing blinders. She refused to look, even though she was curious to see if Scott's truck was in the driveway. As she jogged down the steep gravel hill, she was thankful for a job to do that would keep her mind off Scott. He had called on her late one evening, but she refused to see him.

"What would you have me tell him?" her mother had whispered at Sarah's bedroom door. "He knows you're home."

Sarah was in bed, reading a book. "I don't care what you tell him." She licked her finger and turned the page. "I'm not coming out."

"She's sleeping, Scott," she'd heard her mother tell him at the sliding glass door. "I'll tell her you came by."

Sarah refused to listen to any of his excuses or apologies. She had already been made a fool of once this summer when she caught Hugo kissing Shannon. Her plan was to spend the rest of the summer concentrating on her writing and her job. She was going to avoid Scott at all costs.

Sarah found a large fallen birch tree near the mica

mine. It appeared to have been on the ground for a while, which would make harvesting the bark easier. She took a utility knife from her pocket, sliced vertically down the center, and peeled the bark away from the tree trunk. Once she had more bark than she could carry, she headed home.

Back at the cottage, Sarah found Mabel slipping wildflower seeds into tiny brown packets.

"Since we already scattered most of Daddy's ashes in the ocean, I thought we should have a releasing ceremony for his friends and family here," Mabel said. "They can release the seeds after the burial."

Sarah smiled. While the funeral in B.C. had been painful, Sarah felt her dad's burial at the cottage was going to be a celebration of his life. She was happy to be a part of creating something special to honor his memory.

The next morning, Julie arrived bright and early just as she had promised. She brought her guitar with her after Sarah had suggested that Julie should play the music at the ceremony.

"I'm nervous," Julie said, passing Sarah her suitcase from the trunk.

"You never get stage fright," Sarah said walking toward the cottage with Julie's luggage.

Julie stopped in her tracks. "This is more than a performance, Sarah. Your dad was like a second father to me."

Sarah put Julie's suitcase down on the carpet of pine needles and wrapped her best friend in a warm embrace. "That's why we asked you to do this," said Sarah. "Having you sing and play at the ceremony will make it more meaningful."

Sarah had been right. There wasn't a dry eye at the ceremony as Julie gently strummed her guitar and sang *Over the Rainbow*. The priest kneeled beside her father's grave and lowered the wooden urn into the ground. Everyone took the seeds from their packets and released them into the gentle summer breeze. Next year, the grave would be surrounded by a colorful wildflower garden.

The cemetery was small and didn't have a parking lot. The dirt road alongside it was lined with cars. A white picket fence surrounded the cemetery, protecting the well-tended lawn and rows of crooked headstones. Many graves dated as far back as the 1800s.

Sarah had been so focused on making sure the ceremony ran smoothly that she hadn't noticed Scott's presence until it was over. He stood in the back with Jeff and his parents. Sarah saw them for the first time when Julie skipped past her to say hello to Jeff. Jeff picked Julie up and twirled her around. Sarah looked past the happy couple and locked eyes with Scott. She felt a tug in her chest, as though her heart was breaking all over again. She was thankful to have another excuse for the tears that dripped down her cheeks.

"It was a beautiful celebration of your dad's life," Mrs. Roberts said to Sarah, wrapping her in a motherly hug. "Your dad would be so proud of you."

Sarah forced a smile. "Thank you for coming," she said to the entire Roberts family. "It means so much."

Jeff gave Sarah a sympathetic smile and kissed her on the cheek. "I'll go help Julie get her guitar and music stand to the car."

Mr. and Mrs. Roberts moved on to pay their respects to Sarah's mother and Mabel, leaving her alone with Scott. He had his hands in his pockets and rocked forward and backward on his feet.

"I know I'm probably the last person you want to see right now." Scott's cheeks puffed as he sighed through pursed lips. "Your dad was an awesome guy, and

I just wanted to pay my respects. I'm sorry if—"

"Don't apologize. He would've wanted you to come. I'm glad you did."

"Listen, Sarah, I wanted to tell you—"

"No explanation needed, Scott. I—"

"Damn it, Sarah!" Scott pursed his lips together. He lowered his voice to a whisper. "After all we've been through together, I thought you'd at least give me a chance to—"

"This isn't the time or the place, Scott. So, if you'll excuse me."

Sarah walked past him, but it felt as if she were dragging her feet. Her legs were as heavy as lead. Even though Scott had hurt her, she still felt pulled to him like a magnet. It took all her willpower not to turn around. She tried to ignore the guilt that crept in. Maybe she should have listened to what he had to say. She sighed, taking one last look at her dad's final resting place. She opened the passenger side door of her mom's car and collapsed into the front seat. She knew she didn't have it in her to listen to Scott explain why she wasn't good enough to love.

The next morning, Sarah tiptoed around her room in search of her lifeguard uniform. The pine floor creaked under her feet. Julie stirred in bed.

"What are you doing up so early?" she moaned.

"I have to go back to work today," said Sarah, slipping her green shorts overtop her one-piece bathing suit.

Julie sat up in bed and rubbed her eyes. Her pixie cut stood on end. "Do you think that's a good idea?" Her tired hazel eyes showed concern. "You buried your dad yesterday."

"I've already taken a week off for his funeral. Besides, I need the money for school." Sarah pulled her long hair into a sleek ponytail. "Do you have plans to see Jeff today?"

Julie stretched her arms over head and nodded. "He's taking me out on their boat."

Sarah smiled. Even amid her heartbreak, she was happy for her best friends. Sarah leaned over the bed and pecked Julie on the cheek.

"Have fun!" she said, racing out the door. If she didn't get moving, she'd be late for work. She didn't want to suffer the wrath of Kurt.

Sarah felt a sense of relief as she passed the Roberts' driveway. Scott's truck was parked in the laneway, which meant he probably wasn't working the same shift as Sarah. One less awkward encounter for her to face that day.

She rolled all the windows down, and the car filled with the crisp morning breeze. Sarah caught a whiff of August on the air and was instantly transported back to a sweet summer morning with her grandmother. She could still feel the cold sand between her toes as she searched for frogs along the edge of the lake.

"There's a green frog!" her grandmother had whispered, handing Sarah a net.

Green frogs were Sarah's favorite because their call reminded her of the sound of a banjo. She snuck up behind the frog and quickly snatched him into the net. Her grandmother filled a plastic pail with lake water, and Sarah plopped her catch into the makeshift aquarium. She kept the net overtop the pail to prevent the frog from escaping. She searched the beach for stones and shells, wanting to create a frog paradise for her new friend. When her grandmother told her it was time to release the frog back into the lake, Sarah had cried. At only seven years old, Sarah had a hard time comprehending why she couldn't keep the frog as her pet.

"We must keep nature wild, Sarah," her grandmother had said firmly but lovingly.

Sarah turned the car into the empty public beach parking lot. Before rolling up her windows, she took another deep breath. Sarah felt it comforting to know that even after someone you love died, the seasonal carousel continued to spin.

Sarah was the first employee to arrive that day. She grabbed her keys from her backpack and unlocked the staff changeroom. She stuffed her bag into her assigned locker and read the calendar that was posted on the staff bulletin board. Scott was not scheduled to work. Relieved, she went to the adjoining ladies' room to splash cold water on her face. Suddenly, she heard Shannon and Britney's voices. She quickly turned off the tap and patted her face dry with a brown paper towel.

"I still can't believe he got fired," said Shannon.

Sarah's ears perked up. She tossed the damp paper towel in the trash bin and stood at the door, eavesdropping.

"He should've never laid his hands on me," said Britney.

"The scumbag deserved it."

Sarah had to know who they were talking about.

"Who got fired?" she asked, stepping back into the changeroom.

"Kurt," Shannon said. She shut her locker door and slipped a red whistle around her neck. "The creep got handsy with Britney."

Britney nodded, pulling her green uniform shorts up over her matching one-piece bathing suit. "I never would have reported him if it wasn't for Scott," she said, tying the white drawstring into a bow.

"I imagine it must have been hard to talk about. What did Scott say?"

"He didn't say much. He listened. Scott never made me feel like it was my fault, and he supported me in turning Kurt in. He's such a great friend."

"You mean, you and Scott aren't back together?" Sarah asked.

"Gosh, no. He made it crystal clear earlier this summer that he is definitely not into me."

"But the other night at the dock, I—"

"I know what that must've looked like. I'm sorry I didn't say anything. I was distraught and embarrassed. I didn't know who to turn to."

"I was the one who encouraged her to talk to Scott," said Shannon. "He's senior staff, and I thought he'd know what to do."

Sarah looked down at her feet. She couldn't believe what she was hearing. She had been so wrong about Scott. Her stomach ached from the guilt that suddenly consumed her. She felt ashamed. She watched as Britney pulled her hair into a messy bun. She was in awe of her strength for having come forward.

"I'm so sorry about what happened to you, Britney."

Britney smiled at Sarah. "I have to admit, it felt damn good taking that creep down."

Sarah laughed. It felt odd to connect with Britney over their shared experiences with Kurt.

"Scott is amazing, Sarah. You're lucky to have him," said Britney.

Sarah felt her heart drop into her stomach. She had made a huge mistake that she didn't think she could rectify. She was terrified Scott would never forgive her.

"Come on, ladies!" Shannon said swinging open the door. "Our shift is about to start, and I heard our new boss runs a tight ship!"

Sarah's shift dragged on. As she fit yet another

child into a lifejacket, the thought of faking sick crossed her mind, but she didn't want to make a bad first impression with her new boss. Amanda was a large woman with thick thighs and a chest so big she wore a sports bra underneath her swimsuit. Shannon had been right. Amanda was a strict manager, but she also had a hearty laugh that was endearing. Despite being unable to get Scott off her mind, Sarah pressed on. She tirelessly taught families how to enter canoes safely, restocked the first aid kits, and took her turn keeping watch on top of the lifeguard tower.

At the end of the day, Sarah changed into her jean shorts, applied a layer of watermelon scented deodorant under her arms, and slipped a fresh white t-shirt over her head.

"We're headed to Fiddleheads for drinks and appetizers," Britney told Sarah as she changed into a Barbie-pink summer dress. "Do you want to come with us?"

Sarah thanked her for the invitation and made up an excuse about having to get her mom's car back at a certain time. The truth was, she was desperate to find Scott and apologize. She couldn't think of anything else.

The short car ride back to the cottage felt like an eternity. She turned up the radio and peeled a piece of Big Red gum out of its silver wrapper and popped it into her mouth. She blew a cinnamon flavored bubble as she revved the car up the steep gravel hill to their cottage. Sarah's heart deflated when she saw that Scott's truck wasn't in the driveway. She wondered if she might find him if she turned around and drove to the lookout. In the end, she decided against driving around aimlessly and felt it best to wait for him at home. She parked her mother's car in the laneway, grabbed a blanket from the back seat, and headed straight for the dock.

The sun was beginning to set, and Sarah smiled at its beauty. She loved how the sky never looked the same. Every sunset was a unique work of art. The horizon was a warm yellow line painted across the sky and reflected into the lake below. The top of the canvas was streaked with bright pink brush strokes that blended into the yellow, making a gradient in the evening sky. The background score of birds chirping and cooing gave Sarah goosebumps. She felt absolute peace in the presence of such beauty. If only she had someone to share this incredible moment with.

"Sarah?"

She turned to see Scott standing at the bottom of the stairs. Her heart skipped a beat and she stood up to greet him. Scott looked handsome in a pair of jeans and an olive-green t-shirt that made his eyes pop. He had perfected the art of messy curls.

"Listen, I know you've made it clear that I'm the last person you want to talk to, but I need to tell you something. I never—"

"I know you didn't," Sarah said, walking toward him. "Scott, I owe you an apology."

"I'm the one that needs to apologize." Scott took Sarah's hands into his. "Given my history with Britney, I know what the other night must've looked like. I'm truly sorry. I should have explained the situation right away."

"I didn't even give you a chance," Sarah said, squeezing his hands. "Besides, it wasn't your story to tell."

Sarah stared into his soft, inviting eyes. The hurt expression from the past few days had disappeared.

"Sarah, I would never do anything to intentionally hurt you."

Sarah looked away. Intentional or not, it was painful knowing Scott might not feel the same way she felt about him.

"Hey." Scott's fingers cupped her trembling chin, forcing her to make eye contact. "You can talk to me, you know. What's going on?"

Sarah took a deep breath. She needed to know how he felt, even if what she was about to hear might hurt her deeply. "I'm thinking about how much fun I've had with you this summer, how much I'm going to miss you in the fall, and I'm wondering how you feel about me?"

Scott's mouth twitched with amusement. "Spending time with you has been the best part of my summer."

"Really?" Sarah asked, her voice full of hope.

"Really. There was a time when I refused to let myself think about you that way because I was worried I would screw everything up and ruin our friendship. Sarah, I can't fight these feelings anymore. There is no one else I want to be with. I'm in love with you."

Sarah's heart sang with delight. "You love me?" she stuttered. She needed to hear him say it again to confirm she wasn't imagining things.

Scott nodded. "I have loved you for a long time."

One step, and she was in his arms. When his full lips gently pressed into hers, Sarah melted against his body. She kissed him back, releasing years of pent-up passion. She loved feeling the warmth of his skin. The heat rose to her cheeks as his tongue playfully explored her mouth. Time felt as though it had stopped, but the tickle in her chest intensified. Their first kiss was everything she had imagined it would be. It was the sweetness of their childhood and the promise of years to come.

"I love you, too," Sarah said, looking into Scott's kind eyes.

His lips formed into a satisfied grin, and he pulled her back in. Scott kissed her again, hungry and lovingly, and her whole body tingled.

"I don't want this summer to end," Sarah murmured. She buried her face against his neck. "How will we make this work?"

"Kingston is only a few hours from Montreal. I could drive up once a month to visit you and you could take the train to come see me on long weekends. We'll call each other every day. Sarah, I want to make this work. I've never been happier."

Sarah sighed with contentment. She knew Scott had given their situation a lot of thought and she felt they could make a long-distance relationship work. "And we'll always have summer," she replied, thinking of all the years they had spent together at the cottage since they were young.

They stood at the end of the dock, wrapped in each other's arms, watching the sun set behind the pine trees. Just when Sarah thought there couldn't be a more perfect ending to the most romantic evening, she heard the whimsical call.

"Look, Sarah, the loons!" Scott said.

But it was his face she looked at first.

So charming was his wonder.

The End

ACKNOWLEDGEMENTS

It only takes one 'yes'! A heart full of thanks to Stacey Adderley for accepting my debut novel at Evernight Teen. I would like to thank my wise editors Carrie Clauson and Corinne DeMaagd and mentor, Laurie Clayton, for their patience, constructive criticism, and encouragement. A special thank you to Evernight Teen's Laura Baird and to my talented cover artist, Jay Aheer, for creating the book cover of my dreams.

Thank you to my parents, siblings, and closest friends for reading through the first draft of *Summer at Pine Lake* and encouraging me to keep writing.

My deepest appreciation goes to my mother, Meg, for everything.

Thank you, always, to my best friend, Jerin Forgie. I love you like a sister.

Oceans of gratitude to Dad, Caleigh, Patrick, Isaiah, Uncle Mil, Justin, Emily, my author friends, and grade six teacher, Mrs. Beanish.

To every reader who has picked up this book: thank you, thank you, thank you!

To my amazing children, Henry, Rosie, and Hubert, thank you for surrounding me in a love like no other and for teaching me to believe in magic.

I want to thank my incredible husband and love of my life, Mike, for always encouraging me and making it possible to chase my dreams. With you in my life, it was easy to write a happily ever after!

Last, but never least, I want to thank my guardian angels, Grandma, Nannie, and Uncle Peter.

ALYSSA DELLE PALME

Alyssa Delle Palme is a radio host, who has packed away her microphone, but her passion for storytelling has brought you her debut novel, *Summer at Pine Lake.* Her news, sports and entertainment stories have been heard over Canadian airwaves coast-to-coast. Alyssa is also the Director of a non-profit nature school, Wild Roots. When Alyssa isn't writing, she can be found adventuring in the forest with her three children, Henry, Rosie, and Hubert.

ALYSSA DELLE PALME

Evernight Teen ®

www.evernightteen.com

www.ingramcontent.com/pod-product-compliance
Lightning Source LLC
Chambersburg PA
CBHW030545200626
46810CB00027BA/1095